P9-CCW-095

ESCAPE
ROOM

ESCAPE ROOM

MAREN STOFFELS

Translated by LAURA WATKINSON

Underlined

This is a work of fiction. Names, characters, places, and incidents either are the product of the author's imagination or are used fictitiously. Any resemblance to actual persons, living or dead, events, or locales is entirely coincidental.

Text copyright © 2017 by Maren Stoffels
English translation copyright © 2020 by Laura Watkinson
Cover art copyright © 2020 by Sean Gladwell/Getty Images

All rights reserved. Published in the United States by Underlined™, an imprint of Random House Children's Books, a division of Penguin Random House LLC, New York. Originally published in paperback by Leopold, Amsterdam, in 2017.

Visit us on the Web! GetUnderlined.com

Educators and librarians, for a variety of teaching tools, visit us at
RHTeachersLibrarians.com

Library of Congress Cataloging-in-Publication Data
Names: Stoffels, Maren, author. | Watkinson, Laura, translator.
Title: Escape room / Maren Stoffels ; translated by Laura Watkinson.
Other titles: Escape room. English
Description: First American edition. | New York : Underlined, [2020] | "Originally published in paperback by Leopold, Amsterdam in 2017." | Audience: Ages 12 and up. | Summary: Told from multiple viewpoints, Alissa, Sky, Mint, and Miles enter an Escape Room with one hour to find clues, crack codes, and solve puzzles, but the Game Master has no intention of letting them out.
Identifiers: LCCN 2019055656 (print) | LCCN 2019055657 (ebook) | ISBN 978-0-593-17594-1 (trade paperback) | ISBN 978-0-593-17595-8 (ebook)
Subjects: CYAC: Escape room games—Fiction. | Interpersonal relations—Fiction.
Classification: LCC PZ7.1.S7527 Esc 2020 (print) | LCC PZ7.1.S7527 (ebook) | DDC [Fic]—dc23

The text of this book is set in 11-point Sabon MT Pro.
Interior design by Cathy Bobak

Printed in the United States of America
10 9 8 7 6 5 4 3 2 1
First American Edition

Random House Children's Books supports the First Amendment and celebrates the right to read.

Penguin Random House LLC supports copyright. Copyright fuels creativity, encourages diverse voices, promotes free speech, and creates a vibrant culture. Thank you for buying an authorized edition of this book and for complying with copyright laws by not reproducing, scanning, or distributing any part in any form without permission. You are supporting writers and allowing Penguin Random House to publish books for every reader.

For Annemieke, because you're always there,
even when you're on the other side of the world

If you had one shot, or one opportunity,
to seize everything you ever wanted
in one moment,
would you capture it,
or just let it slip?

—Eminem, "Lose Yourself"

THIS

IS

WHAT

HAPPENED

BEFORE

I can see It from here.
It can't see me.
It has to pay.
For everything.
All I need is a sign.
Please.
Give me a sign that I can begin.

MINT

"He's gay. For sure." Sky's sitting on the backrest of the bench, right behind Alissa and me. It's just the three of us. The rest of the park is deserted.

"Don't think so." Alissa takes out her wallet. "How much do you want to bet?"

I have no idea who my two best friends are talking about. Their conversations often pass me by, like I'm on the other side of a wall.

Alissa waves a five-dollar bill around. It reminds me of the first day of junior high. I thought Alissa had made a bet then too.

She came up to my desk that first morning and asked if the seat next to me was taken. Alissa was the kind of girl who could have sat anywhere. She was so incredibly beautiful. Her eyes were the color of the sea on the Italian coast, where I'd spent the summer. I looked around suspiciously. Where were her giggling friends, laughing at me from a distance because I'd fallen for it?

But there was no one else there. We were the only ones in the classroom.

Sky's voice brings me back to the present. "Let's bet for a pizza," he says. "And Miles can deliver it. Perfect."

So they're talking about Miles, who works at the pizzeria with Sky. I've never seen him before, but Alissa's mentioned him a few times.

A girl with blond hair and a red scarf around her neck comes jogging into the park. As she passes us, she flashes me a quick smile.

"He's on his way, so now we just have to wait and see." Sky puts his phone in his pocket and casually rolls a cigarette. He never has actual packs of cigarettes. Sky always does everything just a little bit differently from everyone else.

"Did it hurt?" I hear Alissa ask. I'm back on the bench in the park. What were they talking about now?

I follow Alissa's gaze to Sky's eyebrow piercing, which he had done a while ago. When he turned up at school the next day, the skin around the piercing was red and swollen. I touch my own eyebrow, which also hurt for a few days.

At first I thought it was a coincidence, but then when Alissa broke her wrist in gym, mine was painful for weeks too.

Can I feel other people's pain? Is that possible? It feels supernatural, weird. And if anyone finds out, I'll get even more of a reputation for being crazy.

Sky points at his eyebrow. "So much gunk came out! I could have made it into a smoothie."

Alissa gives him a shove and he nearly falls off the back of the bench. "Stop! You're going to scare me out of it."

Since when has Alissa wanted a piercing? I try to imagine what it would look like on her, a little ring through her eyebrow.

A couple weeks ago in Textile Studies, we had to make

dresses out of garbage bags. Alissa pulled hers over her head, grabbed hold of it on one side, and shot a staple through the plastic. Then she paraded around the classroom like she was on a catwalk. Some of the boys started whistling. Even in a garbage bag, she was stunning.

"Where's that pizza?" Alissa asks impatiently.

"Miles has half an hour to get here. After that, the pizza's free."

A few minutes later, a scooter with a big blue trunk on the back drives into the park.

Sky grabs my wrist and looks at my watch. "Bang on time. Typical Miles. You see? He's a punctual gay guy."

My stomach's churning, like I'm about to take an important exam.

"Stop it." Alissa quickly straightens her T-shirt. It's a small gesture, but I can tell she's nervous.

Miles brakes in front of our bench and gives Sky a wave. When he lifts the visor of his helmet, I see two bright-blue eyes, like Alissa's. But there's something cold about these eyes. They have nothing to do with the Italian sea, but are more like icy water. I get a weird feeling that I can't quite identify.

"One pepperoni pizza?" The boy takes out a pizza box. The scent of melted cheese makes my mouth water.

"Yep. It's for us." Then Sky points at Alissa. "She's paying."

"You think?" Alissa looks at the boy. "Hey, Miles."

MILES

I don't like it when people know my name and I don't know theirs. Feels like I'm down 1–0.

I've seen this girl before. She meets Sky after work sometimes. I noticed her immediately because she has the same blue eyes as me. Dad used to say I was the only one except him with blue peepers like this, but he was wrong. This girl's eyes are hypnotic.

Did Sky tell her my name?

The girl smiles. "Want a slice?"

I hesitate, because I really need to get going, but something about her voice makes me stop.

It's only then that I notice the other girl on the bench. She's leaning forward slightly, with her straight hair hanging over her face like two curtains. She doesn't quite seem to belong.

"It's almost time for your break, isn't it? Come on, have some." Seems the girl with the blue eyes knows not just my name, but my work schedule too.

I can see part of her bare neck.

What would it feel like to kiss that soft bit of skin?

I'm startled by my own thought. After Karla, I made up my mind never to feel anything for a girl again. It's easier to reject them all than to let anyone get close. Because when they get close, they start asking questions. Questions I can't answer.

I know I should go, but somehow I find myself taking off my helmet and sitting down beside her.

"Here." The pretty girl passes me the box. As I eat my slice, I dare to sneak a closer look at her. There has to be something about her that's disappointing, something that'll help me to forget about her later.

But her voice sounds like she's singing. Her eyes are an endless blue. And she smells like autumn sunshine.

I'm not sure I want to forget her.

I swallow the pizza. "And who are you?"

ALISSA

We're sitting so close that Miles's leg is touching mine. He's looking at me as if he hopes to find something in my face. His eyes scan every inch of my skin.

I've never talked to Miles, but whenever I go to meet Sky at work, I watch him from a distance.

Miles stands out, not because he's good-looking, but because he doesn't seem to want to be. It's as if his looks torment him somehow. And that's something I recognize.

Boys like to check me out, and it drives me crazy. Andreas is the last boy I kissed, and I really did like him. But after our kiss, I heard him bragging about it like I wasn't even a person, just some "hot" girl.

Sky's handsome too, but his rough-and-tough exterior scares a lot of people off. Which seems like a great idea to me.

At home, I sometimes stare at myself in the mirror. I don't dare get a tattoo, but how about a piercing? Once I put a dot on the side of my nose with a Sharpie. The thought of a stud in my nose instantly made me feel stronger.

"And who are you?" asks Miles.

"Alissa."

"Are you gay?" Sky asks.

I get why the teachers say he's direct. He's like a bulldozer sometimes.

Miles shakes his head irritably. "No, I'm not gay."

Sky lights his cigarette. "No need to get pissed. Gay people are cool."

Miles puts the last bit of pizza into his mouth and stands up. "Got to go."

Is he leaving because Sky asked that question? I realize that I'm riled up. I want Miles to look at me again the way he just did. It was like he could see much more than my exterior.

"Sky's paying for the pizza," I say. "And the tip."

SKY

I curse to myself.

Alissa likes him.

I thought this was just about a bet, but Alissa smiled at Miles the way only she can. Her boy-slaying smile.

When I get home, I turn the amp for my electric drum kit up high. Drumming always works, but not this time. Even after playing for half an hour, I still feel angry. I pull off my headphones.

Why can't I shake it off?

Alissa doesn't have a clue that I only started dating Caitlin to divert attention.

Caitlin's in our year at school. If I squint, they even look a bit like each other. But Caitlin's blue eyes don't match up to the real thing.

I fall back onto my bed and look at the group photo on my nightstand. Having it there makes it hard for me to sleep, but it's even harder without it.

I pick up the photo and hold it close to my face. There's a small worn patch where I sometimes press my lips to it. We're standing close together, our arms touching.

I'd really like to cut everyone else out of the photo, but this way Alissa can come into my room without realizing what's up. There's no need to worry about Mint. She spends half her time floating in another dimension.

"You belong with me," I say quietly to the photo. "You just need to see it."

ALISSA

"You coming?" I ask Mint as she gets on her bike.

"Where to?"

"To get the piercing?"

"Now?" Mint smiles. She knows I have no patience. When I have an idea, it has to happen right away.

"Of course."

"What do you think?" I ask yet again when we're both on our bikes.

"Nice." Mint went so pale as the needle sank into my nose. It was like she was the one who was suffering.

A few minutes later, we're riding our bikes into the upscale neighborhood where Mint lives. The first time I went to her house, I couldn't believe my eyes. But Mint's dad is a lawyer, so he obviously earns way more than my dad, who works for the fire department.

At the door, Mint reaches for her keys, but the light in the hallway goes on and her mom opens up.

"Where were you?"

I know Mint's mom can get, like, totally panicky, but it still shocks me every time. She talks to Mint like she's a little kid. My younger sister's nine, and not even she gets treated that much like a baby.

"Mom . . ." Mint blushes.

Mint's mom gives me a quick nod but then turns back to her daughter. "A deal is a deal."

My dad's already in his firefighter uniform when I come into the hallway.

"What's that in your nose?"

I turn my face from left to right. "Do you like it?"

Dad tries to look stern, but then he bursts out laughing. "I think it's cool. Hey, your mom will be home soon. Ruben and Koby are upstairs. Will you give Fenna a hand with her math homework?"

"Sure."

He kisses me on the forehead and closes the front door behind him. I watch through the glass as he rides his bike out of the front yard.

When I was little, I used to spend hours awake in bed, waiting for my dad finally to come back safe from work. I didn't dare close my eyes until he was home. Sometimes I didn't manage to stay awake. Then I'd wake up with a start in the middle of the night and run barefoot to my mom and dad's room. When I saw the lump on his side of the bed, I'd sneak back to my room, feeling relieved.

These days I do sleep, but never very deeply.

Certainly not since last Christmas.

One night, when Dad was on duty, four people died in a fire, including one of his fellow firefighters. A beam burned through and collapsed on the guy's head.

The people who lived in the house were in the bedrooms on the second floor, and no one could reach them. Dad tried to get through, but it was too dangerous. In the end, all he could do was stand and watch helplessly as the whole house burned down.

Absolutely none of it was his fault, but the accident still changed him. Dad stayed home from work, wandering around the house like a ghost. Even the firefighters who'd been with him that night couldn't get through to him.

Dad used to scream the whole house awake. Nightmares, Mom said, but that was an understatement.

Fenna would climb into my bed, terrified, whenever Dad started screaming. I'd hold her until she fell asleep.

I hated that Fenna had to go through that. I really wanted to do something to help, but I didn't know what.

So when a documentary maker asked me if I'd do an interview about the effects of the fire on our family, I said yes immediately. The documentary was broadcast on a kids' channel, and I hoped I'd be able to help someone, even if it was just one person.

It got loads of positive reactions from all kinds of young people, which pulled me through that tough time.

The situation with Dad seemed to be going on forever, but at a certain point it gradually started to get better. They gave him medication to calm him down. He saw a psychologist and, with the help of the other firefighters, he was even able to go back to work for half days.

After a few months, he went back full-time and seemed to have forgotten it all.

But I haven't forgotten.

Now and then I watch the documentary again. I see the dark circles under my eyes, which look anxiously into the camera.

Even now, I still feel that scared sometimes.

MILES

Alissa. Every pizza I deliver for the rest of the evening, I'm thinking about her. As I ride my scooter home, I can still see her bare neck.

I don't realize where I am until I'm almost at the front door. This is my old street.

How is that possible? All this time, I've never gone the wrong way. I settled into our new place immediately.

My heart skips a beat when I see that nothing's changed. The sidewalk is lower in one place, where I could always ride over it on my bike without bumping the back wheel.

In the window of number 39, there's still a line of wooden cows on the ledge. I used to spend ages looking at them when I was a little kid. Dad stood patiently beside me as I counted them and gave them all names.

The memory's painful.

Nothing's changed here, and yet *everything* has changed.

"Hey, sweetie," Julie says as I go into the kitchen. "How was your day?"

Should I tell her that I accidentally rode my scooter to our old street? But then she will ask me all kinds of questions: how that made me feel, if I'd like to go visit the grave, if I want to go back to the old house with her. . . .

"Oh, it was okay." I lean over the pan. "Smells good."

"Want to set the table?"

I put the plates opposite each other. Even though it's just the two of us, Julie always cooks. She's never allowed herself to be defeated after we lost Dad. But I know she cried over him for many nights. I could hear it through the thin walls of our new apartment.

I tidy the pens on my desk, stack the books I have to study for my driver's license, and push my chair in.

It's pitch dark outside; inside too.

I'd like to turn on the light, but then Julie will know I'm not asleep yet. Last week she asked if I often have trouble sleeping. I don't know what she wants from me.

Does she want to see me cry?

I eat, drink, move, but nothing feels real anymore.

Until this afternoon.

Alissa felt real.

Now I'm thinking about her *again*.

I lie down on my bed and turn my head to one side. I'm staring directly into my wardrobe mirror. I often hang something over it, but it's not covered now.

I see my hair, my lips . . . the looks that have helped me so often. People in grocery stores are always extra friendly.

Teachers help me out if my grades are falling a little short. And girls will do just about anything for me.

But my face isn't going to bring anyone back.

And what about Alissa?

Can she fix anything?

I think about Karla, the last girl who was in this room. She lay with me on this bed, under these sheets.

We talked about the future.

What we wanted to do, what we wanted to be.

Because we were sure we were going to get old together.

I had a future with her, but I destroyed it.

And I'll destroy Alissa too.

I need to stay far, far away from her.

The light's been off for a while.
It must be asleep by now.
Without any nightmares.
I'm the one with the nightmares.
Over and over and over.
And every time the same.
I turn around,
because I can't stand here all night.
Today I finally got what I was hoping for.
There was such a slim chance
that this must be the sign.

SKY

On Friday afternoon, I'm happy when I can finally leave school. I know I shouldn't be mad at Alissa, but I still am.

She's in love with the wrong person. Why can't she see that?

I head into the employees-only section at the pizzeria and, as I'm putting on my apron, I spot a flyer on the table.

Curious, I read the words.

SUPER-REALISTIC ESCAPE ROOM!
THE HAPPY FAMILY

THE DOOR SHUTS.
YOU HAVE SIXTY MINUTES.
BUT WHERE WILL YOU START LOOKING?

FIND THE CLUES! CRACK THE CODES! SOLVE THE PUZZLES!
CAN YOU ESCAPE WITHIN AN HOUR?

BUT BE WARNED:
THIS IS NERVE-RACKING, BLOOD-CHILLING, HEART-STOPPING!
NOT FOR THE FAINT OF HEART OR THE FEEBLE OF BRAIN!

THE HAPPY FAMILY IS DESIGNED FOR GROUPS OF AT LEAST 4 PEOPLE.
(THIS ESCAPE ROOM IS TERRIFYINGLY TENSE!)

I read the flyer three times to let it all sink in. The word "super-realistic" has sucked me in. I always think the haunted houses at the county fair are ridiculously fake, but this? This is something I have to do.

Maybe, just maybe, just for a moment, I'll forget the photo on my nightstand when I'm in this Escape Room. And maybe I'll forget that those blue eyes will never look at me the way I want them to.

"Shouldn't you be working?"

I turn around and see Miles. He points at the flyer in my hand. "What's that?"

I'm mad at him too, maybe even more than I am at Alissa. Those longing looks he was giving her yesterday. I just can't bring myself to look at Caitlin that way, no matter how hard I try.

I stuff the flyer into my jeans pocket. "Nothing."

Alissa and Mint are waiting outside when I leave work later. Alissa's piercing twinkles away at me. Like she wasn't pretty enough already.

"You coming to the movie?" Alissa asks.

"Got a date with Caitlin." The moment I say it, I feel nervous again. Recently I've had the feeling that Caitlin wants to go further than just kissing. I know I should want the same, but I can't do it. My mind's on someone else.

"Things are pretty serious with you two, huh?"

I make a strange noise that could mean anything. A quick change of subject.

"Want to go here next Friday?" I pull the flyer for the Escape Room out of my pocket.

Alissa frowns. "What is it?"

"Oh, I've heard about that!" To my surprise, Mint pulls the leaflet out of my hand. "You have to solve puzzles so you can escape."

"And that's your idea of fun?" Alissa raises an eyebrow.

Mint nods. "Sounds cool."

Alissa exchanges a quick glance with me. She's clearly thinking the same thing I am: Mint's too timid to do anything. She usually stays at home when we have a school trip, and Alissa and I go to the fair on our own every year because Mint says the rides make her nauseous. She rarely visits me at work, always claiming she has a stomachache or headache.

"Fine by me," Alissa says.

I point to the bottom half of the flyer. "We just need a fourth person."

"Caitlin?" Mint suggests.

Being with Caitlin already feels like one big real-life Escape Room.

"Or Miles?" Alissa says.

I curse to myself. No way I want to spend sixty minutes watching those two getting closer.

"Then there'll be four of us." Alissa looks at me. "Shall I ask him?"

* * *

I'm lying with Caitlin on my single bed. There's a movie on the TV, but I'm hardly taking in anything about the plot.

Alissa asked Miles to come with us, and so on Friday next week I'll be locked up with the two of them for an hour.

How could I be so dumb? Why did I even mention the Escape Room?

"That was good." Caitlin yawns and stretches. I only notice now that the credits are rolling. I completely missed the end of the movie.

"How about we go to sleep now?"

I look up, startled. "We?"

Caitlin hardly dares to look at me as she whispers, "I brought my pajamas."

I knew this was going to happen, but I'm not ready.

Caitlin disappears into the hallway, into our bathroom. I have to think of something, but what? I've already told her twice that I wasn't feeling good.

Caitlin comes back in wearing a nightgown made of some kind of shiny fabric. It looks new. I wonder if she bought it especially for me.

"Are you going to sleep in your jeans?" she asks.

Oh yeah, that's right—my clothes need to come off too. I get off the bed and pull down my jeans, but keep my T-shirt and boxer shorts on for safety.

Giggling, Caitlin climbs under my comforter. "You coming?"

Maybe it's like bad cough medicine: sometimes just downing it in one gulp is the best approach.

I turn off the light and feel my way to my bed. I'm surprised by how soft Caitlin is. Soft legs, soft arms, soft stomach.

"So here we are, then," I say.

Caitlin takes my hands and puts them over her breasts. I can feel her stiff nipples through the fabric of her nightgown.

I realize I should be doing something, so I start kneading them on automatic pilot as if they're made of pizza dough.

Caitlin's hand slides down and she feels between my legs.

No, no, no. This shouldn't be happening. This can't be happening.

I hear the front door. My mom and dad are back from their night out with friends.

"Hey, my mom and dad are home," I say. "We can't do anything now. Their bedroom's right next door!"

It's quiet for a moment, and then Caitlin whispers, "Too bad."

I hold in a sigh of relief. For now, I'm safe.

"Yeah, too bad."

Caitlin cuddles up close to me and puts her head on my chest. Before long, she's snoring quietly, with her leg over mine.

It's hours before I fall asleep.

Not long to wait, and then it'll be Friday.
Friday. Free day.
And finally I'll be free.

MILES

I said yes.

I'm going with Alissa to the Escape Room. What else was I supposed to do?

I can't get her out of my head. On Monday, I think I see her walking through town. I race after her on my scooter, but it turns out to be someone else.

On Tuesday, I find the documentary she's in on the internet, and I watch it five times in a row.

Wednesday night, I dream that I'm kissing her and wake up with drool on my pillow.

On Thursday, the waiting's driving me crazy and I tear through the meadows on my scooter. When I open the visor of my helmet, the fresh fall wind hits my face.

I have to stop this. Nothing's going to happen between me and Alissa. It's doomed to fail.

In the middle of the meadows, I brake and kick down the stand. I pull the helmet off my head.

There's a bench just like the one in the park where I met Alissa last week.

At first, I hoped I was just making her prettier in my head

than she really is. But every time I paused the documentary, her blue eyes looked deep into mine.

Karla used to look at me like that when we were still together.

Whenever I think about Alissa, I automatically think about Karla.

That last time, she looked at me like I was a stranger. She was terrified of me. And no matter what I said, I couldn't make it up to her.

It's going to end just as dramatically with Alissa, maybe even worse.

I can feel this huge rage bubbling up inside me.

Why can't I just get on with my life? Why does everything from back then keep chasing me around like a swarm of wasps?

I swing my helmet backward with a big sweep of my arm and thump it onto the bench a few times with a succession of dull thuds.

I shatter my memories into splinters.

MINT

I've had stomach pains all week, someone else's stomach pains. I can't think who they're coming from, but they're getting worse every day. By Thursday afternoon, it's like I swallowed a razor blade. When I'm out cycling in the meadows, I actually have to stop for a moment and clutch my stomach with both hands.

I groan as another stabbing pain shoots through me. What on earth is this?

Then I'm startled by a scream somewhere very close to me. My view is blocked by a big bush, but as I walk toward the sound, I see a boy standing by a bench. He slams a helmet onto the wood twice, three times.

Then he hurls the helmet away, and it rolls into a ditch. A couple of ducks fly up into the air, terrified.

I'm about to get back onto my bike, but then I see who it is. Miles.

He slumps down onto the bench and covers his face with his hands. Is he crying?

My stomach's suddenly so painful that I have to bite the inside of my cheek to stop myself from screaming. I double over behind the bush and breathe deeply.

So now I know who the pain's coming from. What's wrong with Miles? My nose was hurting last week because of Alissa's piercing, but that was nothing in comparison. My stomach feels like I'm being ripped open from the inside.

Someone's approaching in the distance. A woman. As she gets closer, I see it's the same jogger from the park last week. I recognize her by the red scarf.

She's reached Miles now, and she stops in her tracks. What's she going to do? She'd be crazy to talk to Miles when he's so mad.

But then I hear her quietly asking him something. She probably wants to know if he's okay.

Miles takes his hands away from his face and lashes out at her. "What the hell do you want?"

I back away. The woman does the same. I hear her saying something else, but I can't make out what it is.

"No!" Miles's voice sounds really furious now. "You heard me, didn't you? Get the hell away from me!"

The woman runs on, and I stand there behind the bush, frozen. Why was Miles yelling at a stranger like that?

I think about Alissa, who seems to like him. I'm sure she'd change her mind if she saw that.

I look at Miles, who is staring into the distance. In the park, he didn't even introduce himself to me, as if I was invisible, but being invisible does have its advantages.

I make myself scarce.

* * *

30

Alissa is just coming out her front door when I get there. "Hey, what are you doing here?"

All the way to her place, I've been debating with myself what I should do, but the bad feeling I got about Miles made my mind up for me.

I take a deep breath. "I'd just like to talk to you for a moment."

Alissa grabs her bike, which is leaning against the front of the house. "Now? What about?"

"About Miles."

"Oh, well, speak of the devil. He just sent me a message to ask if I wanted to go over to his place for dinner so we can get to know each other a bit better before tomorrow."

It's like a hundred alarm bells going off in my body at once. "Don't go," I blurt out.

Alissa frowns. "Why not?"

I have absolutely no evidence against him. It's more of a hunch. There's something about Miles, something that's not right.

That look in his eyes—it gives me the shivers.

But is that enough to convince Alissa to cancel her date?

"Just be careful, okay?"

Alissa bursts out laughing. "With Miles? I know who you got that panicky stuff from, but seriously, you're being a bit of a drama queen."

* * *

31

I look at myself in the mirror and see two big green eyes. Alissa's remark hurts. I know my mom panicked last week because I was late, but that's bad enough. Alissa doesn't need to compare me to her.

And at the same time I'm wondering about it. Is that how everyone sees me?

I look at my reflection again. The girl who looks back is nondescript, a nothing. Alissa is exactly the opposite. You *have* to look at her, whether you want to or not. Sky's also pretty striking, with his piercings and the clothes he wears, but me?

I'll never forget Sky coming to sit in front of me and Alissa on the first day of school.

"He's got to be a drummer," Alissa said to me. "Want to bet?"

Before I could even answer, she'd tapped Sky on the shoulder.

"You a drummer?"

"Yep." Sky looked closely at Alissa. "So what do you play? No, wait, you're a singer, aren't you? You're pretty enough to front a band."

It was a simple remark, but it made me feel invisible. Like I was not much more than Alissa's shadow. And it kept on happening after that. Why do I let them do that? I saw the way Sky and Alissa looked at each other when I reacted so enthusiastically to the Escape Room. They weren't expecting that from me. Mousy little Mint, who's scared of everything. Well, I don't want to be that Mint anymore. The Escape Room feels like a new beginning. And a new beginning calls for a new look.

I bunch my hair together and hold it up. Now that it's out

of my face, I look completely different. More open, as if the curtains in a theater have finally gone up.

I dig around in my desk, looking for the makeup kit my aunt gave me for my birthday one year.

The green eye shadow is the same color as my eyes. I draw a line with the eye pencil and put on mascara.

When I step back to take a look at myself, I get a shock. This girl might not be a supermodel, but she's not invisible anymore.

I feel an energy flowing through my body that's stronger than my fear of being noticed.

This is who I can be—at least if I stop hiding.

MILES

Alissa will be here any minute.

I sent her a message right after what happened in the meadows. I couldn't take it any longer.

I don't want to wait until tomorrow. I want to see her *now*.

Julie was surprised when I said someone was coming for dinner. She wanted to know who, and I said it was Alissa.

"Alissa? Is she your girlfriend?" she asked.

I shook my head. "Not yet."

Julie smiled. I think she was relieved. She wants nothing more than for me to move on with my life.

The bell's ringing. My heart skips a beat.

Alissa's here.

ALISSA

I can't help it. All the way to Miles's apartment, what Mint said is on my mind. Why did she come to warn me about him? Maybe I should have asked more questions, but I was already late. Besides, Mint's just like her mom. They both get all panicky about stuff.

Trying to put her remark out of my mind, I ring the bell of the last apartment. The door swings open almost immediately, and Miles is standing there with a flushed face.

"Hey, you're here! Come on in."

I follow Miles to the living room and kitchenette, where a woman shakes my hand. She's younger than I'd imagined Miles's mom would be, but he looks so much like her. They have the same smile, a smile that their eyes join in.

"So you're the girl Miles has spent an hour in the kitchen for, are you?"

Miles cooked for me? I smile to myself. My last thought about what Mint said dwindles and fades away.

While Miles is getting the dish out of the oven, I look around. The living room is small but cozy. There are some photos on the bookshelves. My eyes linger on a photo of a man who is practically Miles's double. It must be his dad.

I look at a photo of Julie with a friend outside a café. They both have huge ice cream sundaes in front of them.

"I love desserts," Julie confesses when she sees me looking.

There's another picture of a blond girl around Fenna's age, and a few of Julie and Miles together.

"He's a good-looking guy, huh?" Julie sounds so proud that I can't help laughing.

"Sure is."

It's kind of strange being here, but Julie makes me feel welcome. It's like Miles and I have known each other for months.

Behind us, Miles puts a steaming dish on the table. "Dinner's ready."

There aren't any photographs in Miles's room. Actually, there's hardly anything in there, just the bare essentials. He does have a keyboard, though.

"You play the keyboard?" I ask curiously.

"A bit." Miles sits down on his bed. "My dad gave it to me."

"Um, where is your dad?"

"Dead."

"Oh . . ." I can feel my face turning red. "I . . ."

"You had no way of knowing." Miles's face becomes hard, as if he's wearing a mask. "Did you?"

"No." I wish I could take back my words. It suddenly feels so uncomfortable. The good feeling I had during dinner has melted like snow in the sun.

"How . . ." I weigh my words carefully. "How long . . . ?"

"Almost a year now." Miles looks at the floor. "We used to live somewhere else."

I look around. That explains why Miles's room looks so sterile. They must have just moved in.

Miles pats the bed beside him. "Come and sit with me."

I feel my heart beating faster as I drop down next to him. We're sitting close together, like on the bench last week, but this time Mint and Sky aren't watching.

"Weird, huh?" I say, but don't dare to look at Miles. "Us sitting here like this."

"Do you think?"

"Not really," I admit. "It feels kind of familiar."

Silence for a moment. I don't know what else to say. The clock above his door ticks the seconds away.

"Your dad was sick, wasn't he?" Miles says, and it's like he just stabbed me. That's how shocked I feel.

"How . . . How do you know that?"

Miles blushes. "I watched the documentary."

Two things go through my mind. First I feel angry, as if Miles has seen something that wasn't meant for his eyes. But then I start to feel warm inside, because it means he looked me up online. If you search for my name, the documentary is the first thing that comes up.

"My dad had PTSD," I say.

Miles nods. "That must have been hard."

Sky and Mint have seen the documentary too, but we've

never really spoken about it. Sky's no chicken, but he's not much of a talker. Mint just kept giving me worried glances, like she thought I might collapse at any moment.

But Miles has just brought it up like it's the most normal thing in the world. And he was honest about *his* dad, so I want to be honest about mine too.

"My little sister started sleeping with me. She was too scared to sleep alone, because Dad screamed in the middle of the night. When I was small, I used to sleep badly when he went to work, and I'm still having problems with it now, after the accident. It's like every day I'm just . . ."

"Frightened," Miles says, finishing my sentence.

"Yes." I turn to look at him. Miles's bright-blue eyes are sparkling, as if there are thousands of little lights in them. "I've never talked to anyone about this."

"Except for in that documentary," Miles says.

"Exactly." I smile. "I don't think my friends dare to ask me about it."

"I know that feeling." For a moment, I'm afraid that Miles's hard mask will come back, but that doesn't happen.

"What's it like with your friends?" I ask.

"Don't have any."

At first I think Miles is joking, but he looks deadly serious.

"Don't you like people?"

Miles shrugs.

"I'd have thought you had loads of friends."

"Why?" Miles points at his face. "Because of *this,* right?"

"A bit," I admit.

38

"I *hate* it."

I can feel myself smiling. Wasn't that exactly what I'd thought I'd seen in him?

Miles sighs. "Whenever I meet people, they have an instant opinion about me. Oh, I bet he's arrogant. Oh, I bet he has stacks of girlfriends at the same time. But I've only ever had one girlfriend."

MILES

Why did I start talking about that? I could kick myself, especially when Alissa asks "What was her name?"

"Karla."

Saying her name out loud makes it feel like she's here, just for a moment.

"When did you guys break up?"

I'll never forget that day, but I pretend I have to think about it.

"January."

"After your dad . . ."

"Yes. I wouldn't talk about it, and she couldn't handle that."

That's not true. The problem was that I *did* talk about it. And I can never take back the things I said.

I remember the moment Karla's father appeared at the apartment, soon after Karla ran away. He yelled at me to stay away from his daughter. Said he'd drag me straight off to the police if I ever tried to see her again.

Thank goodness Julie wasn't at home at the time. She's always thought I was the one who broke up with Karla.

"What about you?" I ask quickly. "You got any exes?"

"Nothing serious." Alissa blushes a bit. "With me, boys are often after only one thing."

"Sex," I say. "I get it. You're beautiful. But there's more to you than that."

Alissa nods slowly. That piercing in her nose is new, I think. My eyes are drawn to the stud. And then they automatically move to her mouth.

I want to kiss her.

The skin under her ear, her neck, her stomach . . .

What would she do if I leaned in? Maybe it's too fast, too much. The evening's gone so well. I don't want to ruin it now.

But then she kisses me.

My stomach explodes as I pull her closer and feel her soft tongue sliding against mine. She kisses so differently than I remember Karla kissing.

Karla . . . If Alissa knew what I'd done, she'd never kiss me like this.

I push that thought away. I should be enjoying this. The past is over.

Alissa's hand goes up and into my hair. I'm back on my old bed, in my old room. Karla often used to brush my hair the wrong way, giving me instant goose bumps on my arms. Which always made her laugh.

I pull away. A reflex.

Other images shoot through my mind. The creaky stairs that always gave us away when Karla wanted to slip out in the morning before my mom and dad realized she'd slept over. Dad teaching me how to play chess and patiently explaining the rules for the tenth time.

"What's wrong?" Alissa's face is so close that I can't see her clearly. "Don't you want me to touch your hair?"

My throat feels dry, as if I haven't had anything to drink for hours.

Alissa smiles. "My brothers don't let me do it either. Koby gets really mad if I mess up his hair. And my dad's hair is sacred, even if he is almost bald."

My dad had dark-brown hair, the same as me. I look like him. Whenever I see myself in the mirror, I see him. And then I'm hit by the stone-cold realization that he's under the ground somewhere. My face brings Dad so close to me every day, but it will never bring him back.

I don't want Alissa to talk about her dad. It makes me think about mine.

"Come here," I say, pulling Alissa toward me again.

I want to go on kissing until the bad feeling's gone. And even then I don't want to stop.

I want to believe that we'll make it together, even if it's just for now.

ALISSA

For the first time since Dad's illness, I've *really* talked. Miles asked about Dad, and I answered. It was that simple. Why did Sky and Mint never try doing that?

All the way home on my bike, I'm deep in thought. I dared to kiss Miles.

I didn't think about it, just leaned in. At first I was afraid he'd push me away, but then he actually pulled me toward him. We kissed like we had years of catching up to do.

Everything with him happens so naturally. I become a version of myself I don't recognize, but one I really like.

Just be a bit careful, okay?

But why? The only scary thing was Miles's face when he talked about his dad. But what do you expect? If my dad died, I'd go mad with grief. I don't know if I'd ever be able to talk about it normally. I can hardly even talk about when Dad was sick.

I pull the front door shut behind me. All the lights in the house are already off. Everyone's asleep. I head for the living room, because there's no way I can sleep yet. I'm way too hyper about Miles and our kiss. I'll see him again tomorrow, but it feels like I'll have to wait forever.

In the darkness, I see a figure sitting on our sofa, so someone is still awake.

"Dad?"

I switch on the small lamp next to the TV.

"What are you doing in the dark?"

I take in the scene, from the untouched bowl of chips on his lap to the absent look in his eyes.

I feel my heart racing.

This looks a lot like when . . .

Should I get Mom? But then it'll start all over again. The worried look in Mom's eyes is almost harder to bear than the vacant look in Dad's.

"I was just thinking."

Dad's voice sounds bright and clear. It's a relief. When he was sick, he sounded so far away.

"What about?"

"Come over here and sit with me." Dad puts his arm around me. I see our reflection in the black screen of the television. Dad in his firefighter's uniform, me still in my coat.

My dad starts talking. "A teenage girl got seriously burned tonight. She wanted to make a fire with her friends, but it got out of hand. Someone saw the blaze and called us. I even spoke to the girl for a second before they carried her into the ambulance."

"What did she say?"

"She thanked me. I think she was completely high from the adrenaline. She called me a hero."

"And that's exactly what you are," I say.

My dad cringes, and I immediately regret what I said, because I know he's thinking about last Christmas. The little girl who died in the fire was the same age as Fenna is now. The fire took four lives that night.

I cautiously look at him. Does my dad still think it was *his* fault? That makes no sense at all. The investigation proved it: there was absolutely nothing he could have done. If he'd gone back into the house, I wouldn't have a dad now, like Miles.

"Daddy?" Fenna appears in the doorway. When she sees us sitting there together, her face clouds over. "Are you crying?"

My dad shakes his head. "No, baby girl. Daddy's not crying."

"I'll take her to bed," I say, quickly standing up. The last thing I want is for Fenna to start worrying. But as I tuck my little sister in, she looks at me with fearful eyes.

"Daddy's shipwrecked again, isn't he?"

It feels as if my heart breaks into a thousand pieces.

Tomorrow.

THIS

IS

WHERE

THE

DOOR

CLOSES

SKY

"Sky!"

This week I managed to avoid Caitlin at school, but now she rides up alongside me.

"What are you doing tonight?" she asks.

"Going to an Escape Room," I say. "With Mint, Alissa, and Miles."

Alissa and Miles. I've had three nightmares about them this week, and all three ended in a kiss. I'm dreading the thought of later, being locked up with the two of them from eight to nine this evening. What am I going to do if they spend the whole hour flirting with each other? Just the thought of it is driving me crazy.

"Hey, cool!" Caitlin looks at me sideways. "Can I come too?"

I could pretend that four people is the maximum, but what if Caitlin looks it up? No, I'll have to come up with something better than that.

"Sure, you can come. I need to go by work first, but if you're waiting outside the Escape Room around nine o'clock, we'll be there too." It's not technically a lie. We *will* be there; we'll just be leaving, not arriving. Then I can tell her I got the time wrong. Or she did.

ALISSA

Dad looks at me in surprise when I walk into the living room with my coat on. "Where are you going?"

"To an Escape Room." I look at my watch. "I'm already late."

"But you were going to babysit for Fenna tonight."

Shit. I completely forgot.

"Can't Koby or Ruben do it?"

"They've gone into town. Your mom's at Janet's, and I have to go to work."

I look at Dad's uniform. Why doesn't he find another job? Something dull in an office, for example, so I know he'll come home safe at the end of the day.

"My friends are counting on me. Can't Fenna stay in on her own?"

"She's nine, Alissa." My dad sighs. He was grumpy this morning too. Probably didn't get much sleep last night. I heard him go to bed, and I'd been awake in my room for hours by then.

"I really can't do it tonight. Tomorrow would be fine, but not now. Mint's going to be here any minute."

My dad shakes his head. "You're staying here. A deal is a deal."

Tears of fury fill my eyes.

"Your dumb job sucks!"

"Excuse me?" My dad suddenly sounds like Mint's mom. He's not usually so strict. Whenever he tries to be, he just bursts out laughing. But not this time. Fenna's right. Dad's changing again.

I'm not sure I can handle this another time.

"You're always at work," I scream. "I hate it!"

My dad's face darkens. "Alissa . . ."

I can't stop. The words I've been saving up for months come pouring out.

"You're the one who should stay in, not me. You go out every night and just expect it all to be okay. Well, it isn't. Do you know how much I worry? And not just me. Fenna has to sleep with me, because she's frightened of you. She cries herself to sleep every night. She's not *my* daughter, Dad. She's *yours*. So damn well behave like a father for once!"

Where is It?

MINT

Something's wrong. Alissa's cycling way faster than normal. I want to ask her about it, but her snappy comment is still fresh in my memory. I'm worried she's going to call me panicky again. If she does, I might just burst into tears.

She hasn't brought it up again, and I haven't asked her about her evening with Miles either.

I told my mom and dad that we're having a movie night at Alissa's. It didn't feel good, but I know they hate things like Escape Rooms and they might have made a fuss. Gotten worried.

As we ride our bikes over there, Alissa still doesn't say a word. I don't think she's even noticed that I'm wearing makeup for the first time in my life.

SKY

Things have changed.

Mint and Alissa don't say a word to each other as they come cycling up. Mint's wearing makeup and she's put her hair up. She looks like a different person.

"Looking good," I say as she locks up her bike.

Mint blushes. "Thanks."

Miles is the last one to arrive on his scooter. He gives me a quick wave and then leans in close to Alissa.

For a moment, I think his kiss is going to land on her cheek, but then he kisses her on the lips.

They mix like watercolor paint, becoming one color.

How did I ever think I had a chance?

"Should we go in?" Mint's suggestion makes Miles and Alissa finally release each other. I try to pull myself together, but it's as if my body is slowly crumbling. All the hope I had is gone.

Mint pushes open the wooden front door and we step into a long corridor, which is pretty dark. The only light is coming from tea lights in holes hacked out of the walls.

Halfway down the corridor, there's a waiting room with a

jukebox and two shabby sofas. On the wooden crate that's serving as a coffee table, there are flyers for the Escape Room.

The adrenaline I felt when I first read the flyer surges through my body again. I have to focus. I'm not going to let those two ruin my evening.

"Where's the staff?" I ask Mint, but then I suddenly hear a voice behind me.

"Good evening." A young woman with platinum-blond hair holds out her hand to shake mine. "I'm Cleo from the Escape Room."

I've been waiting for this moment
for more than ten months.
And now It's standing in front of me, in the flesh.
I shake Its hand.
It has no idea who I am.
I have to use all my willpower not to stare at It.
It's just a player, just like the other three.

ALISSA

I shake Cleo's hand, but I barely look at her. My mind's on Dad, on the things I said to him.

Why didn't he react? It's making me feel guilty, and that's making me even madder.

Mint must have noticed something was wrong, but she didn't ask me about it. Instead, she just rode along beside me, looking completely different. I did notice her makeup, but I don't know what to think about it. I liked the way she's always herself, never tries to be someone else.

"I know you," I hear Mint say to Cleo. "You were jogging in the park last week."

"Maybe." Cleo looks around our group. "Shall I explain the idea to you?"

Then she proceeds to tell us so much that I only remember about half of it. I hear her say that we can buy hints with special coins if we can't work it out, and that she'll be watching everything that happens in the Escape Room on camera.

"What's the record?" I hear Sky asking.

"Thirty-five minutes and thirteen seconds," Cleo says from memory. "And we add extra time for each hint you buy. But believe me, beginners often need them."

*   *   *

We have to leave all our stuff in a locker, and I feel strangely naked as we head down a long corridor and into the Escape Room.

Cleo stops in front of a steel door, which looks like something from a prison. There's a hatch in it, like the ones that guards use to give prisoners their food.

"The Happy Family is through this door. Good luck, guys."

Suddenly I realize what's ahead of us. We're actually going to be locked up for sixty minutes and we have to try to escape. What if there's no bathroom in there? I already need to pee.

Cleo pulls the door open, and Sky steps into the room, closely followed by Mint. Miles is the third to go in, but I stay where I am.

"Something wrong?" Cleo asks me.

I don't know why I'm not moving. It seems like my legs don't want to.

Am I scared? I don't like cramped spaces. In Miles's apartment block, I deliberately took the stairs instead of the elevator, and at home I always pee with the bathroom door slightly open.

Miles holds out his hand. "Alissa?"

He must think I look like an idiot. Mint's already inside. If she can do it, then I can too, right?

"You just got your nose pierced. That sounds way scarier to me," I hear Cleo say.

I let Miles pull me inside.

58

The room is the complete opposite of what I'd expected. We're standing in the middle of a family doctor's office.

Behind me, the door closes and a clock on the wall starts ticking. Fifty-nine minutes and fifty-nine seconds. The Escape Room has begun.

I did it.
I can see It on my screen.
The time has finally come.
Let the game begin.

THIS

IS

WHERE

THE

GAME

BEGINS

SKY

I absorb all the details of the room. This office is, as the flyer promised, super-realistic. In the middle of the room, there's a desk of dark wood with a drawer, but it's locked. There's a rug on the floor and two huge bookcases on the back wall, reaching to the ceiling. By the side wall, there's an anatomical model like the one in our biology classroom at school, where you have to put the internal organs in the right place, but this one is empty.

There's a board on the wall with four names on it with empty sections below, which we'll probably have to fill.

On the other wall, there's a big sideboard, but that's closed too, with two locks.

Where should we start?

I look around. There's a camera in every corner. Cleo said she'd be keeping an eye on us. She predicted that we'd need hints, but I want to put that off for as long as possible. If only to prove the opposite.

"Right." To my surprise, Mint takes the lead. "We'll all look around for five minutes, and we'll put everything we find on the desk."

She pulls a folder out from under the rug. "Here."

It's as if that makeup has changed her inside too, as she starts frantically searching the room.

I take all the books off the shelves, one by one. I leaf through some of them, but don't find anything interesting.

"I think this belongs in that anatomical model." Mint comes and stands behind me, with a plastic lung in her hands.

"Where on Earth did you find that?" I ask in astonishment.

"It was in the pocket of that coat." Mint points at the rack by the door and the long trench coat hanging from it. "So do you think we have to find all the organs?"

"Looks like it."

At that moment, I feel something hard behind the row of books. When I bring it out, it turns out to be a plastic kidney. It feels a bit like when I was little and searching for Easter eggs in the backyard. Whenever I saw that pastel plastic, I always got a tingle of excitement in my tummy.

A few minutes later, all the organs are on the desk. It's a macabre still life.

Mint pops the organs into the model, one at a time. It's clear who out of the four of us paid the most attention in biology class, because she doesn't make a single mistake.

Last of all, Mint slots the heart into position. There's a click, and the dummy's mouth drops open. On the tongue, there's a small silver key. The adrenaline rushes through my body.

"W-wow . . . ," I stammer. "This is cool."

"This key is for the sideboard." Mint opens the first lock. "But we need two of them."

Together with Miles, I leaf through all the books again.

Meanwhile, Mint searches the entire room, from the hollow chair legs to behind the board with the names on it.

When I've searched through the last book, I put it down on a table with a sigh. Nothing.

We've looked absolutely everywhere. So where can the key be?

"Up there."

All three of us turn around at the same moment. Alissa has barely moved since we got in here, but now she's pointing at something above my head.

ALISSA

I know I should be helping, but I can't. Ever since that door closed, it's like something heavy is lying on my chest.

So this is how it feels to be locked up.

I need to stay calm, but the four walls seem to be closing in on me. I know I'm not good with small spaces, but this is so much harder than I'd expected.

I look at Mint, who's searching furiously.

The three of us were supposed to go to the county fair together not long ago, but Mint canceled at the last minute. That's my best friend for you—I had to go on all our school trips without her.

But the Escape Room seems to have given her wings. It's as if she never found anything important enough to join in until now.

I look around, trying to find the second key. My friends have already searched through everything, but from where I'm standing I can see a book on the top shelf of the bookcase. It's not visible from where they are.

"Up there," I say, pointing.

Miles stands on the bottom shelf and manages to grab it. It's a medical textbook, and there's a small compartment cut out of the chapter about burns. A silver key is glinting away inside.

"Good spot," Miles says to me while Mint opens the second lock.

In the sideboard, there are four boxes of medicine, which Mint holds up to the board on the wall.

"We have to link these to the right patients."

I often can't follow Mint. She's so incredibly smart. I frequently copy her notes at school, because they're always right.

"Mommy?"

There's a girl's voice in the room, so clear that it's as if she's standing behind me. I spin around, but there's no sign of anyone. Of course not, the voice is coming from the intercom next to one of the cameras.

"Mommy," says the voice again. *"Will you come play with me?"*

Goose bumps pop up on my arms. This Escape Room really is super-realistic. I look at Mint, who's listening carefully. Sky is staring up at the intercom, open-mouthed, and Miles is frowning.

"I don't have time right now, Lia," a woman's voice answers.

"Why not?"

"I'm working. Go ask Daddy."

We hear footsteps and a door squeaking open and closed. Then it's silent again. Only the clock on the wall goes on ticking. We've been at it for just over six minutes.

"What was that?" Sky wonders out loud.

Mint smiles triumphantly. "It's the story of the Escape

Room. Now we know why it's called the Happy Family. The story is about a family with a daughter. The mother's probably a doctor."

Smart Mint, always grasping everything just a little bit faster than everyone else.

"The voices are a distraction," I say. "The name of the room doesn't matter."

"I think it does . . . ," begins Mint. She always thinks she knows best.

She even thought she knew Miles better than I did. She warned me about him. What was she thinking?

"Don't think so." I snatch the boxes from her. "Let's move on."

Mint picks up the folder from the desk, which was the first thing she found. "The diagnoses of the patients are in here. It says here, for example, that Marie van Hillegom suffers from panic attacks. We need to see which drug goes with that."

Panic attacks.

I can see Dad sitting up in bed. One time I made the mistake of going into my mom and dad's bedroom when he was screaming. He looked completely wild and was thrashing around like someone was attacking him. My mom yelled at me to go away, but I stood frozen in the doorway.

"Diazepam," I mumble.

Mint looks up in surprise. "What did you say?"

Did I say it out loud? I don't want to talk about this, but Mint holds up one of the four boxes, with *Diazepam* written on it in big letters.

"How did you know that?"

Dad had bottles of pills on his nightstand. They calmed him down, but made him kind of groggy too, as if my dad was somewhere deep inside, but would never come back again.

All that time, I wanted to talk to my friends, but they never asked me about it. Even tonight, when I came out with my eyes all red and puffy, Mint didn't say a word. She accuses Miles for no reason, but she won't talk about my sick dad. Why not?

"I read it somewhere."

MILES

I look up at the intercom, where the voices were just coming from. The little girl's voice cut straight through me, like she was standing right here in the room.

What else is in store for us?

"So what's the code?" Sky says, fiddling with the lock on the desk. The boxes are in the right order for the patients, but it turns out that it's not the entire puzzle.

"Maybe we should use the first digits of the barcodes?" Mint suggests.

"Nope. It's not that either, Mint," I hear Sky say a little later.

Mint sighs. "We're going to have to buy a hint. This is taking too long."

Mint. So that's her name. Since I got here, she's looked at me a few times. No, more like stared. I hate it when people do that. It reminds me of the psychologist Julie insisted I go see.

Julie thought it would do me good, but the conversations didn't work. The half-truths I told were no use to the psychologist. I don't share my inner self, not with anyone.

What about Alissa? Yesterday, in my room, I told her more

than I meant to. She's getting dangerously close to me, but at the same time it felt good. I felt less alone.

"Fine, we'll get one hint." Sky reluctantly gives me a coin.

When I put it in the slot, nothing happens at first, but then there's a rumbling sound. A plastic ball drops out of the chute and I catch it just in time.

My heart is thumping away like crazy. It looks like one of those gifts from a gumball machine, which Dad sometimes used to buy me when I was small. I was always delighted and usually too excited to get them open. Dad never helped me right away though. He let me sweat for five minutes first. And when he managed to get the ball open after the five minutes, I was even more delighted.

I can feel tears burning in my eyes. How can a dumb ball summon up such a powerful memory?

"What's inside it?" Alissa's voice brings me back to the Escape Room.

I can feel that Mint's still keeping an eye on me. Why is she staring at me like that? Does she think I haven't noticed?

Nervously, I twist the ball open, and I read the note out loud:

The four boxes make a nice set, but don't forget the alphabet.

I don't get it, but Mint's eyes open wide.

"The alphabet, of course! That code game we used to play. The letter A stands for one, B for two, and so on. So Diazepam stands for four, and the drugs are . . ." Mint looks at the boxes. "The code's six-eight-four-two."

I don't think anyone quite understands how she arrived at that code, but when Sky puts it in, the lock springs open.

"And we have . . . this." Sky holds up a handle, the kind that's normally used to wind an awning up and down.

"What are we supposed to do with that?" Alissa sighs. She's less enthusiastic than her two friends. I really thought she wasn't going to come in. I literally had to drag her through the doorway.

"I think it goes in here." Mint points at a hole in the side of the bookcase on the right.

Sky inserts the handle and starts turning. At first, all we hear is creaking, but then the whole rear wall swings aside, including a framed certificate from a first-aid course.

MINT

I'm looking down a long, badly lit hallway. There's a single lightbulb hanging from the ceiling, and I can make out three doors.

Three new Escape Rooms.

That means three new rooms full of puzzles. Searching for three times as many solutions.

I keep a sly eye on Miles. My stomach is way less painful than it was yesterday, but it feels like the pain might come back at any minute.

He was acting really strangely just now with that ball, like he might burst out crying. Did Alissa and Sky notice that too?

Sky tries the door on the right and the door opposite us, but they're both closed. The door on the left does open though.

It's a typical little girl's room, with brightly colored lights, a disco ball on the ceiling, and a loft bed. Two ballet shoes are hanging from the mirror above the dressing table.

"This must be Lia's room." The way the pieces of the puzzle are coming together is addictive. Too bad we only get sixty minutes, because I could spend way longer exploring this Escape Room.

"So what are we looking for now?" Sky says.

There's no sign of locks of any kind in here. The whole room is accessible, including the drawers in the dressing table, which simply slide open.

"There must be a key to the next room in here somewhere," I say, peering around the room again.

Then, without meaning to, my eyes meet Miles's. His bore deep into mine, and I feel a flash of pain in my stomach. I want to look away, but it's as if I'm attached to him.

"Mom? Where are my ballet shoes?"

Lia's voice makes Miles jump, and he breaks eye contact.

"On your mirror, sweetheart!"

"And my powder?"

"In the usual place," says a man. Then the voices fall silent. Cleo only lets us hear scraps of conversations.

"Is this room just a distraction?" Sky says, looking at us.

"I think so." Alissa runs her hand through her hair. She's nervous, particularly since that Diazepam thing just now. She had no trouble matching it to the right patient. She said she'd read about it somewhere, but I'm sure her dad was on that medication last year.

I've watched the documentary that Alissa's in one and a half times now. The first time I missed most of what she said, and the second time I felt so nauseous that I had to turn it off before it finished.

The girl on my screen was a completely different person than the Alissa I know.

Why had she never shown that fragile side to me?

What was I supposed to do about it?

I didn't dare ask about her dad. I was really torn.

Alissa seemed strong, but I could feel her pain. I couldn't stop crying and I had a constant headache. It was *her* sadness, but she wouldn't talk about it.

If she'd shown me just once that she was struggling, then I could have started there, but she didn't. Alissa just remained her old, tough self.

"We'll go look in the hallway." Alissa pulls Miles with her. She didn't listen to my warning.

Yet again, I run my eyes all around the room. The recordings must be a clue. Cleo wouldn't just play them for no reason. What exactly was it that Lia said? She was talking about powder.

There's a black bag hanging from the bed. I open it and see some white powder inside. Isn't that what ballerinas use for sweaty hands?

This is our clue, but what does it mean?

Should I suggest buying another hint? I know it'll cost us more time, but we're wasting time now by going around in circles.

"Ow!" A sharp pain shoots through my hand. Right where my fingers begin, it feels as if someone just drew a knife across my skin.

In a reflex reaction, I throw the bag of talcum powder and it hits the mirror, sending a big cloud of dust into the air.

"What are you doing?" shouts Sky, looking up out of a wardrobe he is searching.

"I . . ." I can hardly say what I felt, can I? I recognize the pain. It's pain that belongs to someone else.

But then the dust cloud slowly settles, and I see the letters in the spots where the talcum powder didn't stick to the mirror. My heart starts beating faster as I read the two words formed by the eight letters: MUSIC BOX.

ALISSA

I take Miles's hand and pull him with me into the hallway, away from my friends.

"Are you okay?" Miles asks when I let go of his hand.

I think about Mint, who's been watching Miles like a hawk since we got in here. What is she up to?

I can't tell Miles that Mint warned me about him. I'm scared he'll think I doubt him too—and I don't.

He's actually really caring. When he kissed me back yesterday, he seemed afraid I might break. I've never had a boy kiss me that gently.

There's an excited shout from Lia's room, where a faint haze hangs in the air.

"What happened here?" asks Miles as we enter the room, but then we see Sky and Mint standing by a pink music box.

There's a familiar tune coming from it.

"Beethoven," Miles says. "It's called 'Für Elise.'"

Sky looks up in surprise. "How do you know that?"

"My mom and dad always used to listen to it."

His dad . . . I'm sure the tune must bring up a thousand memories for him, just as the Diazepam did for me.

Imagine if my dad had died that night. Would I ever have gotten over it?

I take hold of Miles's hand, but before our eyes can meet, the light goes off.

It's pitch dark.

I can't see my hand in front of my face. My breath is racing.

"What's going on?" Sky yells. "Turn on the light!"

I squeeze Miles's hand, but he doesn't squeeze back.

The room feels even smaller in the dark. I've lost all sense of direction. Where was the door again?

The tune by Beethoven suddenly sounds ominous. I wish someone would close the music box.

"Stay calm," Miles says. His voice is so close that it makes me jump.

What should we do if the light doesn't go on again? I feel as if everyone can hear my heart thumping.

"Cleo's messing with our heads," Sky says.

"Do you have a lighter?" Mint asks.

"It's in the locker," Sky says.

I notice that Miles's hand is getting clammy. Maybe he's not as confident as he's acting. "Fire doesn't seem like such a smart plan in here anyway."

I can't see It now.
I can only hear It breathing.
Some people think everything belongs to them.
It's that kind of person.

SKY

Cleo is screwing with us. I know she is. Can't she handle that we've come so far already?

The tinkling of the music box goes on and on.

"Can someone turn off that dumb thing?"

"I can't find it," says Mint.

It's so dark that I start to feel disoriented. Is this part of it? I can't imagine that previous visitors to the Escape Room would have given it five stars if Cleo turned off the light for no reason and didn't turn it back on again.

"Any minute now, that Lia's suddenly going to appear in front of us," I say. "I've heard that some Escape Rooms have actors."

"Don't be dumb," groans Alissa. I'm surprised she's so scared.

I feel around, looking for something to hold on to. I feel an arm, and I grasp it firmly.

"Who's that?"

"Me."

I'd recognize that voice anywhere. The same thing happens inside my body that happened a while ago at the county fair when Alissa and I went on the scariest ride of all. Mint was at home with a stomachache as usual.

Alissa and I sat together in a capsule that was attached to two taut bungee cables. The music got louder and louder, until finally they released the cables and we shot into the air.

At the highest point, I saw the fairground as a small, colorful patch down below. It seemed as if everything was possible up there and, for a second, the world was just as it should be.

The light goes on again. It takes me a moment to get used to the bright glare, and I quickly let go of the arm.

I see that Miles and Alissa are holding hands. If only I could shoot out of here at lightning speed, like in that fairground ride.

Mint closes the music box, and everything is silent. There wasn't a single clue in that box, not a hidden compartment, nothing.

Just as I suspected: this room is a distraction. I realize that I'm getting mad at Cleo. Isn't watching Miles and Alissa bad enough without her having to play games with us as well?

"Hey, how about leaving the light on?" I yell at the cameras. "Or it's not fair, is it?"

Miles puts another coin in the slot. We don't have any other options. This room is a dead end, and there's nothing out in the hallway either.

This time there's a long wait for the ball with the hint inside.

"Any time now would be good!" I shout at the camera. It feels like I'm yelling at Miles and Alissa. It helps me to let off steam. "This Escape Room sucks!"

"What are you doing?" Miles puts his hand on my shoulder, but that just makes me even madder. He's the reason I feel this way. He's destroying everything.

Then a ball rolls into the room. Mint reads the note that's inside:

> You guys are being a teensy bit slow,
> but I'm a nice, kind person, you know.
> So I'll give the next key away,
> at least if you do just what I say.

"This isn't supposed to be some kind of power game, is it?" I look into the camera again. "What's this all about?"

Cleo is playing with us. That much is clear. I didn't like her right from the start. There's something arrogant about her.

Another ball rolls into the room, even though we haven't put in a coin.

Mint reads out the new note. "You have to go and stand by the main door."

"Who?" I jab my chest with my finger. "Me?"

"That's what it says."

I don't understand what's going on. An Escape Room is about solving puzzles, isn't it?

"Just do it." Alissa sounds impatient.

"Okay. I'm going." I head back into the first room, and the others follow. I slide open the hatch in the door and look right. All I can see is the long corridor we came down. It's empty.

"This is the worst Escape Room ever!" I shout. "I'm going to give you one star! Or can you give zero?"

I rest my hand on the edge of the hatch and look back at the others. Miles and Alissa are standing next to each other again, with hardly any space between them. Will I ever get used to it?

"There's no sign of Cleo. I think she's all talk," I say.

At that moment, we hear the sound of metal on metal.

Crouched under the hatch in the door,
I can hear everything.
"This is the worst Escape Room ever! I'm going to give
you one star! Or can you give zero?"
That cuts right through me.
Do they have any idea how long I worked on this?
Everything's just perfect, right down to the
smallest detail.
I stand up and, with all my strength, I slam the hatch.
I hear something crack.

MINT

I feel the same pain as before, in the place where my fingers begin. It's like they've been chopped off. But to my amazement, it's Sky who screams.

I rush to the door and see that his fingers are stuck halfway through. The hatch is cutting deep into his flesh.

My breath catches in my throat.

This isn't some exciting game.

This is real.

I have to open the hatch, even though I don't want to know what Sky's hand looks like.

"Ready?" I ask Sky, who looks deep in shock. Without waiting for his answer, I open the hatch. It makes a slurping sound. Where his fingers were hit by the metal, they're bleeding and dark purple.

Gasping, I step backward.

"Mint . . . ," Sky pants. "Help me."

He sounds as small as Lia. As if Sky's nine years old and I'm the adult.

I look around, panicking. We need something to stop the blood, but what?

Then I remember that we're in a doctor's office. Didn't I see some bandages in the sideboard? I open the doors and take out a roll of bandages and a pair of scissors.

"Alissa." She's standing with her back to the wall. She's staring wide-eyed at Sky's hand and doesn't react to her name.

I have to do this on my own, so I lead Sky away from the door and make him sit down at the desk. In the light, his hand looks even worse. Can I do this? What if I hurt him even more?

"Mint . . ." Sky's counting on me. I try not to look at the ragged edges of Sky's flesh as I wrap the bandage around his hand. Three times, starting between his thumb and forefinger, and then around his wrist and hand. When the bandage runs out, I tie a knot in it. I pull it as tight as possible, and Sky makes a strange sound.

I feel another stabbing pain in my own hand, and I have to look down at it to make sure nothing's wrong.

"Help us!" I shout at the camera on the ceiling. "Sky's hurt. Would you please co—"

Sky puts his good hand over my mouth. "What are you doing? Do you really want her to come in here?"

"Y-you need to go to the hospital," I stutter. "Look . . ."

There's sweat on Sky's top lip. "She was the one who did this."

I give a nervous laugh. "What?"

"Cleo," Sky says. "I caught a glimpse of her face before she slammed the hatch shut."

ALISSA

I can hear Mint saying something, but I can't make out what it is. Sky's hand looks like a piece of meat at the butcher's.

If what Sky said is true, we're in danger. Cleo has shattered his hand. What else is in store for us? We're at the mercy of a psychopath.

I go to the door and lean against it with all my weight. "Let us out!"

Mint tries to pull me away, tells me to calm down, but I lash out. The last thing I want is for her to tell me to be calm. No one should be calm right now.

"Open this door!"

"Alissa . . ."

"You said you knew her!" I explode at Mint.

"From the park." Mint looks at me. "You saw her too, right? She was jogging laps around the grass, and later I saw her in the meadows too."

"We're trapped in here. What else is she going to do to us?" I say.

I look at the cameras. The red recording lights make me furious. The idea that Cleo is watching us while Sky is bleeding like a pig . . . Those cameras need to go. Now.

I take the desk chair Sky was sitting on and roll it under the first camera. I climb onto it.

"Let us out or lose the cameras," I say into the lens. "Without these bitches, you can't see us. So you can't hurt us!"

My heart thumps painfully against my ribs, but Cleo doesn't react.

She has all the power. Inside here, we have absolutely nothing. Our cell phones are in the lockers. We even left our keys and money behind.

I put my hand around the camera and pull. The thing comes away from the ceiling with a cracking sound, and the red recording light goes out.

The screen goes black,
but this time I can't get the light to go back on.
I pull the scarf from around my neck and scream.
I hit myself and bang on the walls.
They have to listen.

MILES

Mint saw me in the meadows. She saw me yelling at Cleo. Is that why she's acting so weird in here? Is she scared of me?

But who's more dangerous? Me or Mint? If Mint tells Alissa about me, I'll lose her. That can't happen. That mustn't happen.

Alissa throws the camera onto the floor, and the lens shatters. She rolls the chair under the next camera. She is completely losing it.

I grab her by the arm. "Don't."

My voice sounds remarkably calm, even though I'm furious inside. "We shouldn't do this."

I don't want to think about what Cleo will do to Alissa if she destroys her cameras. Something tells me that Sky's injury was just the beginning. How could Cleo do something like that? Sky's hand must be broken at the very least.

This all feels like some kind of prank, as if it's not actually real. But then there's a rumbling sound in the chute again. What else does Cleo have to say to us?

Maybe she's sorry and she'll open the door.

The ball rolls into the opposite wall and comes to a stop. No one seems to want to read Cleo's words.

Slowly, I walk over and pick up the ball. With an uneasy

feeling, I take out the paper. I glance at Alissa, but she doesn't look back at me. Just now, in the dark, she was holding my hand so hopefully, but it only made me feel powerless. Maybe it's four against one, but we can't beat Cleo.

"What does it say?" I hear Mint ask.

I swallow and then read out loud: "'If you don't leave the cameras where they are, you'll be stuck in the dark for eternity.'"

SKY

The bandage already looks pale pink in parts. Is the blood coming through?

The pain is making me dizzy.

I'm sweating like crazy. My T-shirt is sticking to my back. I keep seeing Cleo's eyes, just before she shut the hatch. She looked like a doll, with no facial expression.

Who is this Cleo?

And more important: What does she want from us?

Everyone is silent.

The clock on the wall says thirty-five minutes have gone by. It seems ridiculous now that I was worried about something as dumb as breaking the record.

My hand is tingling under the bandage. I have to resist the urge to look, so instead I try to bend my fingers. Not a good idea. I clench my jaw so I don't scream.

"I'm never going to be able to drum again."

Mint's the only one who looks up. "Of course you are."

I know she's only saying it to make me feel better. After all, she saw my hand too.

I feel tears burning in my eyes. Cleo could have done anything to me, but I need my hands and feet. I need them for the rhythms. I have to be able to drum so that I can stay calm. If I can't do that, I'll lose my mind.

"Does anyone know we're here?" Mint looks around the group. "Did any of you tell someone at home where you were going tonight?"

I look at her in surprise. I thought Mint always had to ask permission for everything. "Didn't you?"

Mint blushes. "No, I lied. Said I was having a movie night at Alissa's."

Mint has surprised me yet again tonight. She was amazing when she bandaged my hand just now. She didn't faint at the sight of all that blood. She just got it done. I can't say the same about Alissa and Miles.

"My mom and dad know that I'm out," I say. "But I don't think I told them where I was going."

"My dad knows, but he's on the night shift." Alissa looks down at her shoes. "He won't be home until early tomorrow morning."

Miles sighs. "I just said I was going to do something with my friends."

Mint nods. "So no one will be missing us yet."

That conclusion hits us like a bomb. It's silent again, but all four of us are thinking the same thing: we don't stand a chance.

I wish someone would say something, doesn't matter what. This silence makes it feel as if we've given up hope.

There must be some way out of here, right? There must be someone who can help us?

"Caitlin . . . ," I whisper quietly. "She knows we're here."

Mint's eyes sparkle. "Really?"

I look at the clock, which says a quarter to nine. Caitlin's probably on her bike by now. She's never late.

Mint takes a pen and paper out of the desk drawer and starts to write, hunched over. Even upside down, I can read her neat handwriting.

Careful! Cleo's listening!!!

Mint's right. If Cleo knows that Caitlin's coming here, she'll have an advantage. Caitlin coming will be a surprise, and then Cleo might make a mistake.

Caitlin, the girl I felt nothing for, all those months, might just be the one who saves us.

I take the pen from Mint and start writing. Luckily it wasn't my writing hand that got wounded. Miles and Alissa come over and read the words too.

CAITLIN WANTED TO COME. TOLD HER IT STARTED AT 9

All three of them look at me. I see surprise, relief, and hope. The hope is coming from the most beautiful pair of blue eyes, which paralyze me. Even here, now that we're surrounded by danger, they still have that effect.

Is Caitlin smart enough

Mint looks at me intently.

I know what she's thinking.

If Caitlin doesn't realize that Cleo's dangerous, she'll be in as much danger as we are.

Who knows what she'll do to Caitlin?

I take the pen again.

I HOPE SO.

Caitlin.
That's that girl.
I've seen her around,
when I was watching It.
What are they writing about her?
I check all the cameras, but I can't read the note.
Do they really think they can outsmart me?

ALISSA

I look at the clock, but it's only ten to nine. The minutes are crawling by.

I don't know whether to be happy that Caitlin's coming here. I don't think she can handle Cleo on her own. Caitlin isn't the tough kind. Actually, I've never understood what Sky sees in that girl. They don't go together at all.

I look again at the hands of the clock, but they're moving painfully slowly.

Dad doesn't usually get home until around five in the morning. Might he want to patch things up before he goes to bed? I try to push away the memory of the hurt on his face, but I can't. Dad looked at me like a dog that's been beaten.

"Damn well behave like a father for once!"

I picture Dad going into my room tomorrow morning and finding my empty bed. That is the first place he'll go, but that won't be for another eight hours. Will we be able to survive in here that long?

What's Cleo planning? Does she want to see us suffer?

Mint said she saw Cleo out jogging, but none of us know her personally. Cleo must have some reason for doing this. Or is she just plain crazy?

A horrible din echoes around the room. All four of us jump to our feet.

Mint leads the way to Lia's room, where we all climb into the big wardrobe and close the door behind us. It's a small space. I'm sitting practically on top of Sky and Miles, but the closed door slightly deadens the sound of the fire alarm.

I knew what it was immediately. My dad has to check all the fire alarms at home every day, or he can't sleep. Since the accident last year, it's become an obsession.

"Is there a fire?" I hear Sky ask.

"It's a method of torture," says Mint. "Loud noises can drive people insane."

How come she seems to know everything? She even remembers stuff like that.

In the semi-darkness, she looks serious. The makeup makes her seem older, as if she's over twenty. Why did she dress herself up like that today in particular?

I only know Mint as the girl who wants to be invisible. But why is she so insecure? Mint can do much more than she shows. I've always thought that. In here, she finally seems to be strong, but in an over-the-top, frantic kind of way. The contrast with the Mint I know outside is insane. I don't get it. It feels like my best friend is a stranger.

Above the howling fire alarm, a bell rings.
It takes a second to get through to me,
but then I see a girl on one of the twelve screens.
Caitlin.
She's standing at the door. . . .
I stare at the screen.
What's that girl doing here?
Now I know what they were writing on that
piece of paper.
They knew this was going to happen.
The bell rings again.
"Go away," I plead.
But she doesn't leave.
"Yes?"
Caitlin looks up, surprised.
"Oh, hello. I'm here for the Escape Room."
I look along the street. There's no one else around.
"We . . . we're closed."
"Closed?" The girl looks over her shoulder.
"But that's Sky's bike."

I give her the smile I've been practicing in the mirror
for months.
The smile that fends off every annoying question.
"Then why don't you come on in?"

SKY

The fire alarm falls silent. As suddenly as it started, it stops.

Mint is the first to get up. "I'll go see if it's safe."

No one offers to go instead. Everyone would rather stay inside the wardrobe. It feels like a safe island in a sea full of sharks.

Mint leaves the door open and more light creeps into the wardrobe.

"You okay?" asks Miles. He hadn't said anything about my hand until now. He hadn't even looked at it.

"Fine," I lie. I have to do my best not to look at the bandage, which is now soaked with blood.

"Did it sever your tendons?"

Why did he ask that? I don't want to think about it. Just the idea makes me want to puke.

"I don't know. I can't move my fingers."

Miles's face clouds over. "I'm sorry."

"You don't have to be sorry," Alissa remarks. "It was Cleo who shut that hatch, not you."

Miles looks at his sneakers. "But if I hadn't come along, you guys couldn't have done this Escape Room. You'd have been one player short."

101

Does Miles really think this is *his* fault? I'm mad at him because of Alissa, but he doesn't deserve this.

"If it hadn't been you, we'd have brought someone else," I say quickly.

Mint returns and looks at us with a serious face. "We have to go back. Cleo has a message for us."

Something's wrong. I can tell from Mint's face.

"What's going on?" I ask as Alissa helps me to my feet.

"Just come with me."

In the doctor's office, I see the metal door again, with a trickle of blood running down from the hatch. *My* blood.

I turn my head away, but the image remains.

"There's a new message." Mint holds up a ball.

"Open it, then," Alissa says.

Mint's eyes flash to me. "I've already read it, but I don't know if . . ."

I already know what she's going to say before the words cross her lips. "She has Caitlin."

I feel numb, stunned. My hand even stops hurting for a second.

Caitlin came here because of me, because she thinks she's my girlfriend. And now that lunatic's got her.

This is *our* game, *our* pain. "C-Caitlin has nothing to do with this," I stammer. "She shouldn't be here."

I double over. My dinner splashes onto the floor, and it keeps on coming. I go on throwing up, as if I'm vomiting out my entire body.

With every gasp of air, I call Cleo every name under the sun. No one stops me. The three of them just let me scream. No one tells me to quit it or even rests a hand on my arm. Because they think Cleo has overstepped every boundary: she's hurting someone I love.

But that's not it. I'm flipping out because she's hurting someone I *don't* love. All this time, I let Caitlin believe I liked her. Why? Because I'm scared the truth will come out.

"Let her go," I say to the camera. "Tell me what you want and let her go."

Nothing happens. Cleo remains silent. The clock on the wall says our time is up, but this Escape Room has only just begun.

Is Cleo looking at her screens now? Is she looking at me? Maybe she's laughing. She's broken me, first my hand and now my heart. If anything happens to Caitlin, I'll feel guilty for the rest of my life.

"You lay one finger on her, and I'll kill you." I wipe my mouth. "Do you hear me?"

"Come on." Mint pulls me away. "You need a clean bandage."

"What difference will a bandage make? That woman's going to kill us, Mint."

Mint shakes her head. She remains perfectly calm, even now. How does she do that? We're like rats in a trap.

"Who are you?" I yell at the camera. "What do you want from me?"

Mint forces me to sit on the desk chair and unwraps the old bandage. It's stuck to my hand in places, but it's not painful anymore.

What has Cleo done to Caitlin? Has she drugged her? Hurt her? Or worse?

I squeeze my eyes shut, but then I picture Caitlin in her nightgown. She wraps her soft legs around me. A sign of love for her, a stranglehold for me.

Will I ever be able to put this right?

"Just close your eyes," Mint says quietly. She treats me gently, as if that's what I deserve. She'd be better pinching me and telling me I'm a cowardly bastard. Because that's exactly what I am.

"Cleo?" Now Miles is giving it a try. "You don't want to do this."

Does he really think there's any point talking to that woman?

"You don't want to hurt Caitlin. I know you don't."

Miles must be blind. He saw what Cleo did to my hand, didn't he?

Another ball rolls into the room, but this time there's more than just a note inside. I see something black inside the ball, which falls out when Miles opens it.

It's a lock of hair.

Caitlin's hair?

I feel like I'm about to faint. But I'm still sitting upright.

Miles looks at me, as if he needs my permission to read the message.

"Go ahead," I say in a hoarse voice.

A life in exchange for a bunch of hair —
and it's Mint who'll be sitting in the hairdresser's chair.
While Alissa takes the scissors and snips,
she can give her friend some beauty tips.
We all know Alissa's the fairest in the land,
and it's time she gave mousy little Mint a hand.
Snip snip, Alissa!

Cleo seems to know us very well. She hits us in the places that hurt most of all: my passion for drumming, Mint's looks. How does she know all this?

And then it finally dawns on me what Cleo wants from us. I look at the lock of hair on the floor. A life in exchange for a bunch of hair.

How could I ever have thought that this Escape Room was an exciting game? I was really looking forward to it. Every key we found sent adrenaline racing through my blood.

But this Escape Room is hell. We have no idea where it's going to end, and Cleo isn't finished with us yet, not by a long shot. She's only just begun.

The hair is proof of that. If Mint doesn't do as Cleo says, Caitlin's going to die.

Caitlin won't stop crying.
Just because I cut off a bit of her hair?
I wrap my scarf around my neck again.
Hair grows back.
But some wounds never heal.

MINT

Snip snip, Alissa!

So it seems that Cleo knows what I think about myself. She knows it would be the ultimate humiliation if Alissa of all people were to cut off my hair. She knows I've been living in her shadow since the first day of school. That people only talk to me because I'm with her.

But how does Cleo know?

Is she that good at reading people?

I think back to the park, where she smiled at me as she went by. Later, in the meadows, she turned up again. So that wasn't a coincidence.

"She's been watching us," I whisper. The others look up. "She was there in the park, and later when Miles . . ."

"When Miles what?" asks Sky when I stop in the middle of my sentence.

When Miles flipped out.

"When Miles delivered the pizza."

I feel another sharp jab in my stomach. Miles's pain?

I look at Sky's hand, which I've wrapped in a clean bandage. In Lia's room, in front of the mirror, I'd felt a pain in my own hand. But that was before he . . .

I gasp. All the pieces of the puzzle are falling into place. My wrist didn't just hurt after Alissa fell in gym class, but before, too. My eyebrow and nose hurt before Sky and Alissa had their piercings. My hand hurt before Sky's hand was shut in the hatch.

The pain I feel isn't just a result of other people's pain. It's a warning of pain to come.

"What? Cleo's been stalking us?" Sky says.

Alissa's eyes widen. "When we came in, she said something about my nose piercing. So she knew it was recent! But how could she . . . ?"

"She knows us." Sky looks like he's about to throw up again.

I feel sorry for him. He doesn't deserve this.

I have to do as Cleo says, or Caitlin will be in danger. It's not worth it, is it?

My hair will grow back again.

"Snip snip, Alissa," I say firmly.

Alissa turns deathly pale. "What?"

Did she really think I'd refuse?

"What's more important?" I say. "Caitlin's life or my hair?"

Alissa picks up the scissors I just used for Sky's bandage. Sky pushes back the desk chair. I sit down and clasp my hands around the armrests. The stomach pain flashes through me again, and I'm convinced it's Miles's pain. Should I warn him? But what would I say?

"Are you sure?" Alissa asks.

"Just do it," I say.

Alissa cuts in silence. Now and then, a bit of hair falls onto my lap. The difference between us will soon be huge. It hurts me when boys look at her, but now it feels as if it's Alissa herself who's dishing out the pain. She's mutilating me.

I force myself not to cry. I'm not going to shed a single tear in here. I won't give Cleo the pleasure.

When Alissa finally puts the scissors back on the desk, I look at the floor. There's a carpet of hair, long strands and short tufts all mixed together.

I touch my head and feel the spikes prickling. Shocked, I pull my hand back. I need to know what it looks like, but I'm scared of what I'll see.

I walk to Lia's room and wipe the powder from the mirror with my hand.

For the second time, I see a different Mint. Her cheekbones suddenly look sharp and striking, and her hair is cut short. The girl in the mirror reminds me of a soldier who's recently come back from the war.

Slowly, I realize this is *my* reflection. This is *me*.

I let a laugh slip out, because it suits me. It looks damn good on me.

Sky comes and stands beside me and looks at me in the mirror.

"Whoa," he whispers.

It takes me a moment to interpret his expression, because no one's ever looked at me like that before. It's how boys always look at Alissa.

* * *

We're sitting on the floor in Lia's room, because the office smells of puke. No one says anything. I sneak peeks alternately at Miles and Alissa.

Alissa hasn't said anything since she cut my hair. Miles is avoiding me, as if I have a scary disease. Did he notice when I nearly let it slip about the meadows?

"The flyer for this Escape Room . . . ," Sky says, interrupting the silence. "There was a reason why it was at my work. She led us here."

I get anxious at the thought that Cleo planned all this down to the smallest details. It makes her seem even more dangerous than I already feared.

"We thought it was our own plan to book the Escape Room, but everything was prepared for our visit. Cleo wants to take revenge on us here."

"Revenge? But why? And on which one of us?" I ask.

"No idea." Sky is supporting his hand. The new bandage is already starting to leak too. He's losing too much blood. It needs stitches—and soon.

Should I look for a needle and thread? But I have no idea how to do it. I could just end up making it worse.

"I don't have any enemies," I say. "How about you?"

Sky ponders the question. "Don't think so."

I see Miles again, in the meadows. It was way out of line, the way he yelled at Cleo, but is that any reason for her to want to torture him? Besides, so far, like Alissa, he hasn't been touched.

But I can't shake off the idea that there's something up with him. Miles seems perfect, but that boy gives me the chills.

MILES

Mint is looking at me again. Now I'm sure of it. She saw me in the meadows. She saw me yelling at Cleo. I have to speak to her alone. She has to keep her mouth shut.

Alissa must never look at me the way Karla did just before she ran away from me.

I tried to stop her, but I couldn't. The guy from the next apartment heard the noise and came outside to ask if everything was okay.

All I could do was watch Karla running away from me. It was the last time I spoke to her. After that, everything had to be in secret. I followed Karla on my bike nearly every day. I was there when she ate an ice cream, when she went shopping or to dance class with Peyton. I hated Peyton and her troublemaking. She was the reason for our breakup.

And now there's Mint, who could do the same as Peyton did back then. She could drive me and Alissa apart.

I have to stop her before she shoots her mouth off.

"I think this Cleo must be really sick," Alissa says. "Don't you agree?"

It takes me a moment to realize she's talking to me. I look into her blue eyes and see a very different expression than back then with Karla. Alissa looks at me as if we're on the same team. It has to remain that way for as long as possible.

"Yes," I say quietly. "You're right."

There's a rumbling in the chute. All four of us rush to the doctor's office.

"What's in it?" Sky asks me in a panicky voice. This time it's just a note. No lock of hair.

I unfold the strip of paper and read the words. My scalp is prickling, and it feels as if the whole room is starting to spin. I can't read this out loud. Complete chaos would break out.

"Miles?" Alissa is standing right next to me. I quickly turn away from her, before she can read it over my shoulder.

I have to come up with something, something different than what's written here.

"She, um . . . She wrote: 'Good luck looking for the keys. Maybe there's another way out.'"

Mint seemed shocked when I just suggested that the two of us should go search Lia's room, but I got her to agree. Sky and Alissa are in the doctor's office. I close the door behind us and pretend to search behind it.

What should I do? I can't just start talking about the meadows. First I have to try to find out exactly what Mint saw.

"Do you like cycling?"

Mint looks at me. "What . . . What do you mean?"

"Like, say, through the meadows?" I say, kicking it up a notch.

Mint blushes bright red. She has no curtain of hair to hide behind now.

She saw me. That much is clear. She knows about my scooter helmet and about Cleo.

"I know you saw me," I say. "But you don't need to be scared."

Mint looks nervously at the door. Is she going to call for help?

"Honestly," I say. "I was just a bit angry."

"A bit?" Mint dares to look right at me. I saw how she took care of Sky. She'd do the same for Alissa.

"What happened there is *my* business, not yours."

"If you're with my friend, it's my business." Mint is still looking straight at me. "You screamed at Cleo. Is that the reason we're in here now?"

I feel the note burning in my back pocket. No one can find out what Cleo wrote, and certainly not Alissa.

"Of course not," I say.

"I don't trust you."

Mint will warn Alissa about me. Maybe she already has.

"I don't care." I stare at her. "As long as Alissa trusts me. And she is in love with me."

Mint's eyes narrow. "You are seriously disturbed."

Karla said exactly the same thing to me back then, in the same tone.

I reach Mint in two steps. Fear flashes across her face. See, she's scared of me. I have to use that. It's the only advantage I have. Before I know it, my hand is around her throat.

"Don't go shooting your mouth off to Alissa."

Mint's eyes are open wide. I can see the veins in the whites of her eyes.

"Is that perfectly clear?" As I say the last word, I gently press my thumb into her skin.

"Y-yes."

"Good." I let go of Mint and hear her gasping for air behind my back. I didn't want to do that, but I had no choice.

MINT

There's a war raging in my stomach. Miles has gone, but I can still feel his thumb on my skin. I have to hold on to the dresser to stop my knees from giving way.

Miles isn't just unreliable. He's dangerous.

I hear him talking to Alissa out in the hallway, but I can't make out what he's saying. His casual tone makes me nauseous. How can he put on a different face so quickly? It's not normal. It's . . .

"Hey, Mint?" Alissa comes into the room. "You okay?"

I want to answer, but no sound is coming from my throat. How can I tell her what just happened?

"Are you crying?"

I collapse into Alissa's arms, leaning my full weight against her.

Miles had his hand around my throat. He could have strangled me if he'd wanted to. Could I even have called out for help?

"Shhhh," Alissa whispers. "It's going to be okay."

I have to tell her to stay away from Miles. That's all that matters now.

"It's Miles. He's dangerous."

Alissa frowns. "Are you starting that again?"

Her words flash through my mind. *I know who you got that panicky stuff from.*

Alissa has to believe me. She *has* to.

"He threatened me."

Alissa looks shocked. "Huh? When? Just now?"

"I saw him yesterday. He completely flipped out. He's dangerous, Alissa. He was yelling and smashing his scooter helmet into a bench, and then Cleo came along and—"

"Cleo?" Alissa says, interrupting me.

"She was out running. She asked Miles something, and he . . . exploded."

"At Cleo?"

Why do we keep talking about Cleo? Didn't Alissa hear what I'm trying to tell her?

"He's disturbed," I say quietly. I take a sidelong look at the door. Miles is even more dangerous than Cleo, because he's in here with us. He's a head taller than Alissa and me, and Sky has only one good hand left.

"He grabbed me by the throat. Here." I point at the place where Miles's thumb pressed into my skin.

Alissa frowns. "I don't see anything."

"He didn't squeeze."

As soon as I say it, I realize I don't have a leg to stand on. As Miles said, Alissa is on his side. I've never seen her like this before. She's completely fallen for Miles's tricks.

"How can you be so blind?" I'm getting angry now. "You can see something's not right, can't you?"

Alissa looks at me silently for a few seconds, and then she says, "Are you mad because of your hair?"

"Huh? What?" Does she really think that's what I'm worried about? "Why would I be bothered about my hair?" I explode. "I was already ugly anyway."

"Are you jealous of Miles and me?"

Alissa doesn't know what she's talking about. That has nothing to do with it.

"You're just jealous because you don't have a boyfriend and I do."

I want her to stop.

"Is that why you're wearing makeup? Because you want to be like me?"

"Not everything revolves around you!" I spit out the words. "Sometimes things are about someone else. But you're only interested in yourself. Even when Sky got hurt, you didn't help him."

"I was panicking!" Alissa takes a step forward. "The way you *always* do, with your stomach and your aches and pains. Everyone feels sorry for you, including me. Why do you think I came and sat with you on the first day of school? I felt sorry for you, sad little mousy Mint!"

I can see it again. I had thought Alissa had made a bet. And that was why she came to sit by me. But this reason is much, much worse.

"Better sad than selfish." The words come pouring out, as if they've always been in there but have only just found the way out. "You always want all the attention, even at your dad's expense!"

I know bringing up the documentary is a step too far, but I can't stop. I want to hurt her.

Alissa's face changes. "You have no idea what you're talking about. But you might if you'd ever asked me about it."

I want to take back my words, but at the same time I kind of want to say it all over again.

"Is it any wonder I get all the attention?" hisses Alissa. "And look at the state of you now, with your hacked-off hair."

It's like someone else lifts up my arm and swings it forward. The flat of my hand slaps hard against Alissa's cheek.

At first her eyes are wide with disbelief, but then they turn as cold as Miles's.

THIS

IS

WHERE

THE

TRUTH

COMES

OUT

SKY

They're fighting. As long as I've known Alissa and Mint, they've never fought. And now Alissa's saying that Mint hit her.

I leave Miles and Alissa in the doctor's office and quickly go to Lia's room, where Mint is sitting on the floor.

I crouch in front of her. "What happened?"

Mint doesn't answer. She mustn't give up, not now. Mint is the only one who did anything when my hand was stuck in the hatch. She let Alissa cut off her hair to keep Caitlin out of danger. She's a leader.

"We need you in there." Quietly, I add, "*I* need you."

Mint looks up. She smiles sadly. "Do you feel sorry for me too? For mousy little Mint?"

I think about the way Mint can be in the outside world, with her sagging shoulders and her lank hair. The way she complains about all those nagging little aches and pains.

I don't want to lie to her. She doesn't deserve it.

"Sometimes."

"Alissa says I'm jealous of her, but that's not it."

"Why would you be jealous?"

"Because she has a boyfriend and I don't. Because all the boys like her."

123

"Not *all* the boys," I say.

"Miles, you . . ."

"Me?" Deep inside me, something explodes. All the blood rushes to my head.

"Do you think I didn't realize?" Mint looks at me, shaking her head. "You said she was pretty on the very first day of school."

What's Mint talking about? Did I really say that to Alissa?

"She hates me," says Mint.

"Of course she doesn't." I'm glad Mint changed the subject.

"I hit her."

"I heard something along those lines." Slowly, I feel my heartbeat getting back to normal. "But we're all pretty confused right now."

"Alissa doesn't believe me." Mint gives me a searching look, as if she's not sure she can trust me. "We were talking about Miles."

Miles? I change my position and hear a creaking sound under my feet.

Mint's eyes widen. "Do that again!"

The floor makes a strange sound, as if there's some give in the boards.

Mint pulls up the rug in one movement. You can barely see it, but one of the floorboards is loose.

I look around at Caitlin.
She's finally stopped crying.
I don't understand.
This girl isn't ugly.
Slowly, the pieces fall into place.
I feel a smile on my lips.
This is the perfect oil to pour on the fire.
Time for a new message.

ALISSA

Miles puts his arms around me and hugs me to him. I realize that I'm crying, but I don't know how long I've been crying for.

Mint slapping me isn't even the worst of it. Her words hurt much more. She's never said anything about the documentary, and now she's throwing it in my face.

"Mint says you threatened her."

Miles immediately lets go of me. "What?"

"I don't believe her," I say. "She's gone completely crazy."

Miles runs his hand through his hair. "Well, I did do something. . . ."

It feels like when you miss a step. This can't be true.

"I tried to talk to her about yesterday," Miles says.

"Just talk?"

"Of course." Miles gives me a shocked look. "What did you think?"

Mint's obviously lying. She wants to hurt me, so she accused Miles and brought up my dad.

"I know about the meadows," I say quietly.

Miles nods. "I didn't want you to hear about it, so I asked her to keep her mouth shut. She must have taken it the wrong way."

"Why didn't you want me to know you were so angry?"

Miles smiles weakly. "Why do you think? We're only just getting to know each other!"

I know that feeling. I want to be the best version of myself with him too.

"I was on edge because of my dad." Miles turns his face away. "A few days ago, I accidentally rode my bike to our old street. It was so bizarre to be there for the first time since Dad . . . You know, everything there is the same, but at the same time it's all different."

I think about what my dad was like yesterday. It wasn't like last Christmas, but he was different than usual.

"I know what you mean."

"I think Mint's scared of me." Miles looks at me, worried. "She's been staring at me all night, but without saying a word."

So he's noticed Mint spying on him too. I feel ashamed for her.

We sit down on the floor. I hear Mint and Sky talking in Lia's room. I don't understand Mint. Is she really that jealous of us being together?

"So you didn't grab her by the throat?" I ask, just to make sure.

Miles looks hurt. "Do you think I'd do that?"

I look deep into his eyes. I see the same blue as earlier this week. He's not lying. No one can lie that well.

I sigh. "I just can't believe Mint would make up something like that."

"Friends are shit."

I look at him. "Why?"

Miles laughs, but it sounds anything but happy. "After Dad died, they all said they'd be there for me. Karla too. They wanted to talk to me. They wanted me to cry. But when I finally did, they left. People can't handle sadness. Have you ever noticed that?" Miles looks at me. "Your friends have never asked about your dad either, right?"

Miles's words slowly get through to me. He's right. Sky and Mint have never bothered to ask.

There's a rumbling in the chute. What does Cleo want now? I don't know if I can handle any more of her messages. When is this torment going to stop? I follow Miles to the chute.

He frowns as he reads the message.

"What?" I ask. "Has she kidnapped any more people?"

Miles looks up. "It's about Sky."

"What about him?" I take the strip of paper from his hand and read:

Why did you guys punish Mint that way,
when Sky is the one with a wicked game to play?
His love for Caitlin is fake, not real.
If she knew, how do you think she'd feel?
Sky lies really well, he lies really quick,
and the way he treats Caitlin should make you feel sick.

I look up. "What's this about now?"

Miles shrugs. "Caitlin?"

I read the message again, but the words haven't changed. It's Cleo who's playing a wicked game, isn't it? Not Sky?

128

Is Cleo trying to drive us apart? Well, it's not going to work. Mint might be a bit twisted, but Sky is honest through and through. I know him better than anyone.

"We've got the key!"

I'm startled to see Sky coming into the doctor's office. His new bandage is soaked through, but he looks invincible.

"Is there another message?"

I slowly lower the piece of paper. I can't read this out. I don't want to hurt him. Sky would never lie to me. He's the most honest person I know. If Sky thinks something, he says it. He's a bulldozer, the most direct kid in the class, sometimes too direct, but I can take it when it comes from him.

"She says you're playing a game," says Miles.

Sky frowns.

Do we really have to kick him when he's down? Sky's already been hurt enough, what with Caitlin and with his hand.

Miles clears his throat. "She says you don't really like Caitlin."

When Sky has to talk in front of the class, he is completely in his element. When he stumbles on the street, he makes a joke of it. But now he's blushing all the way down to his neck.

So it's true.

"But why?" I ask.

Sky shifts from one foot to the other. "What exactly does it say?"

I slowly realize that Sky has actually been lying to me. All that time he was with Caitlin, he was playing a game.

Friends really are shit.

"Why are you going out with her when you . . ."

Sky shakes his head, as if this is a nightmare and he really, really wants to wake up. I want the same, but this isn't a nightmare. This is real.

Just now, he was totally panicking about Caitlin. He can't have been acting, can he? I *know* Sky.

"I want . . ." Sky looks at me and then at Miles and back at me. "I can't tell you, okay? Not here."

I've never seen my best friend nervous before, but he can barely get his words out.

"I don't get it," I say. "I just don't get it."

How can Sky have fooled me for all those months? What kind of game does Cleo mean?

"Not here," repeats Sky, and he looks at Miles again. Is he scared of him? But why . . .

Then the penny drops.

I look at Sky. "You're in love with me."

Sky's cheeks just about explode. He even looks like he's sweating.

"No, that's not it."

I don't believe him anymore. It's like his lies are being poured over all my memories.

All those months he was with Caitlin, was he really thinking about me? We've known each other since the first year of junior high, so why did I never notice anything?

I did kind of notice that he never went out with girls, but Sky was always busy with other things. Drumming, working at the pizzeria. And when Caitlin came along, I didn't stop to think about it.

How could I have missed it?

But as far as I know, Sky never flirted with me. He never touched me. Not like Miles does. Sky's managed to keep this hidden for all those years.

Cleo's right: Sky lies really well; he lies really quick.

"You don't get it." Sky's eyes flash back to Miles and then to me. "I'm not in love with *you*."

SKY

I squeeze the key. It's out. The biggest secret I ever had is out.

I don't dare look at the two of them, but I can feel that my words are slowly getting through.

Alissa is the first to say something.

"You're in love with Miles?"

Hearing it out loud is even worse than it just being inside my head. I don't want her to say it, not her of all people.

I want to get away, but there's nowhere to go. We're locked up. Cleo is slowly breaking us.

How did she know? Was it the conversation I just had with Mint?

She thought I was looking at Alissa, but I'm always looking at Miles.

"Of course not." Miles smiles, shaking his head. "Sky's just joking, right?"

I glance at Miles. It's not a smart idea. His blue eyes have the same effect on me as an electric fence.

"No . . ." Miles's expression changes. "Don't be stupid."

In my mind, he reacted differently. When I looked at his photo and told him about it, he was full of understanding.

When our boss took a picture after our staff outing, I made sure I was standing next to Miles. I felt his arm against mine as I stared into the camera. I wanted to look good. This had to be the perfect photo of us together.

Ideally, I'd have cut out the rest of my coworkers, but if Alissa and Mint had seen that photo, they'd immediately know that I felt more for him. This way, Miles could stay on my night-stand.

"You're gay?" Miles looks at me incredulously. "But . . . but you don't look gay."

"So what do gay guys look like, then?" I can hear my voice shaking. "Neat? Tight jeans? Effeminate?"

At first I thought I stood a chance with Miles. In fact I thought that until last week.

As he rode his scooter into the park, I sat up straighter. When Miles is around, I'm always aware of how I move, how I look.

Alissa did the same thing before me, quickly running a hand through her hair. I didn't think anything of it, because, as always, I was thinking about Miles.

The bet was perfect. Thanks to Alissa, I'd finally be able to ask the question I'd wanted to ask for months.

"Are you gay?"

Miles would look up, with those beautiful eyes of his, and say yes.

And then he'd kiss me.

"No," Miles had said in reality. *"I'm not gay."*

Even after that, I was still hopeful. Maybe he was in the

denial phase, like me in the beginning. Maybe I just needed to be patient.

But now that I've told him and seen how he reacted, I know it's not denial. He's disgusted at the thought of me looking at him in that way.

Over the past few months, I've done everything I could to forget Miles. I called in sick. I tried to imagine that he stank or had a disgusting personality that I would eventually discover.

But it didn't work. I want him to be with me the way he is with Alissa. He's caring, attentive . . . and completely out of reach for me.

"So why are you with Caitlin?" Alissa is looking at me like I'm a stranger.

What was I supposed to do? Alissa often used to make it clear that she thought it was weird for me to ignore all that attention from girls. Caitlin was the only one I dared to try it with. She really is okay. Somehow her blue eyes reminded me of Miles's.

Alissa shakes her head. "You used her as a cover."

"So what?!" I yell at her. "What do you care?"

I'd like to do the same as Mint—to give Alissa a slap. It sometimes seems like she has everything. She has no idea what it's like not to have what she's got.

She's my best friend, and at the same time I hate her. She took Miles away from me, even though I never had him.

Does she really think I don't feel guilty about Caitlin? But I needed her. I wasn't ready to come out of the closet. I'm still not ready. Not even now. I don't want the image that people have of me to change.

I turn to go back to Lia's room, but then, to my horror, I see Mint standing in the doorway.

How long has she been there? Long enough to know I'm gay, but she's looking at me very differently than Alissa and Miles. She has her head at a bit of an angle and a vague smile on her lips, as if she's finally solved a tricky sudoku after weeks of puzzling.

Mint knows what it's like to be different from other people. She knows how it feels for Alissa to have everything when you have nothing. Mint lives in her shadow every day.

"Come on," I say to Mint. "Let's go open up the third room."

MINT

Sky's hand is shaking so much that he can't get the key into the hole.

"Give it here," I say quietly. "I'll try."

Sky's in love with Miles. I can hardly believe it. I always thought he liked Alissa. What was I basing that on? That remark on the first day of school? Or because I assumed all the boys liked her?

"Not *all* the boys," Sky had said, but I didn't understand then what he really meant.

It's Miles he's in love with, just like Alissa. So he won't believe my version of what happened in Lia's room either.

The door opens, and we see a masculine room. On the single bed there's a checkered comforter, with a photo of a football team on the wall above. There's a dresser with three drawers and a keyboard in the corner.

There are photos on the dresser, which I study, one by one. A photo of a couple around Mom and Dad's age draws my attention.

"This must be the doctor." I pick up the photo and point at another one. "And that blond girl must be Lia."

Sky doesn't reply. When I look up, I see that he's sat down on the bed, with his eyes closed.

"Are you okay?" I ask.

Sky slowly shakes his head. "It hurts. I'm worried that I'm losing too much blood."

I look at his wet bandage. It needs to be changed, but the new one will be soaked through within five minutes too.

"I want to stitch you up, but I don't know how."

Sky gives me a crooked grin. "Then don't do it."

I sit down next to him. Our thighs touch. He must have felt so lonely all this time. Particularly this week, when Miles fell for Alissa.

"You're still just Sky to me. Whether you're gay or not."

Sky looks up. "I've destroyed everything, Mint. Because of me, Caitlin—"

"Cleo's not interested in Caitlin," I say to reassure him. "She's interested in us."

Sky sniffs, and I can tell he's crying. I want to comfort him. He needs to know that he's not the only one with a secret.

"I feel other people's pain. I can tell when someone's going to suffer pain, because I feel it in my own body. Before Alissa broke her wrist, my wrist hurt. Same thing with your piercings. And your fingers."

There's silence for a moment. What am I going to do if Sky thinks I'm a drama queen just like Alissa?

"Do you see things too?" Sky asks. "Ghosts and stuff?"

I burst out laughing. I can't help it. "No, thank goodness."

"Is that why you stay home with stomachaches so often?"

I nod. "When the older kids had their final exams, I could hardly eat for a week. I felt their nerves, as if they were mine."

"And you can predict it," Sky says. "So you feel it before the other person feels it?"

I nod again. "Something's going to happen to Miles's stomach."

Sky looks at me, startled. "Is Cleo going to hurt him?"

"Maybe."

"We have to warn him." Sky goes to stand up, but I pull him back.

"He'll never believe me," I say.

"You don't know that. We have to—"

"No." I'm shocked by the fierceness of my voice. "I *can't* go to Miles."

Sky doesn't ask any questions. Maybe he's too weak; perhaps he knows how annoying it is when you're pressured to say something you don't really want to say.

"How do you stand it?" Sky asks after a while.

I've already searched the whole room twice. Sky stayed on the bed. His face is going whiter and whiter.

"What, exactly?"

"All the boys falling for Alissa?"

Strangely enough, it doesn't hurt when Sky says it, even though it's the same as what Cleo said earlier this evening.

"You get used to it," I say. "To being a shadow."

"You're not supposed to be a shadow," Sky says. "You can't let it happen."

"It happens automatically." I think about the park last week. Miles ignored me. I thought that was fine. The high wall I stand behind keeps me safe. No one can touch me there.

"That's too bad," Sky says. "You can do so much more than you let on."

What he says touches me. I don't know how to respond, so I press a key on the keyboard, and to my surprise it's connected.

Lia's voice comes through the intercom. It feels like we haven't heard her for hours.

"Will you play for me?"

"Okay," says a boy's voice. Is this his room?

Then there's the sound of a piano playing, very delicately. Every note the boy plays makes me feel warmer. A strong memory flashes back to me.

I'm sitting with my mom and dad in church on Christmas Eve. It's the only day of the year when we go to church. I'm sitting between them. Mom puts some money in the collection box, and Dad puts his arm around me. His arms are long enough to reach around me to Mom.

It's one of those rare moments when the three of us are together, without work, stress, and hassle. Will I ever have another moment like that?

The intercom falls silent.

It seems like an innocent piece of music, but I know that

there's a reason for everything in this Escape Room. Cleo is going to keep on sending us puzzles, even though I'm sure she'll never let us go.

"It's that keyboard." I point at the black-and-white keys. "We have to play something on it."

"But what?" asks Sky.

I think about the clue in Lia's room. We thought the room was just a distraction, but there was more to it.

"The music box," I say. "Beethoven."

Sky looks up, like he's remembering something. "Miles plays the keyboard."

MILES

How could Cleo see that Sky likes me and I didn't, even when it was right under my nose?

I glance sideways at Alissa. Since we've been alone, she hasn't said a word. I think she's on my side, but I don't know for sure.

I want to protect her in here. She has to understand that. She needs to know I'm here for *her*.

"Can you help us?"

When I look up, I see Mint standing in the doorway. It's a moment before I realize she's talking to me.

I'm surprised she dares to speak to me after what happened in Lia's room.

"Can you play 'Für Elise' on the keyboard?" Mint asks nervously.

I think about the keyboard in my own room. It was a present from my dad, but I never play it. I'm afraid it will bring up the memories I'm desperately trying to push away.

"It'll get us into the last room."

Alissa completely ignores Mint. She's lost her two friends, but that won't be enough for Cleo. It won't be long before it's Alissa's turn. . . .

"I'm coming."

141

SKY

Miles is still just as handsome as he was a few minutes ago. How can I ever get him out of my mind when I could draw him with my eyes closed?

I know he has a small birthmark on his right ear. That he likes things to be lined up straight. How many times did he tidy my worktop? Whenever I got back from the bathroom, my knife would be in a straight line with the chopping board, the tomatoes would be neatly sliced and waiting in a row, and the dish towel would be folded over the handle of the oven. Miles does everything perfectly. Miles *is* perfection.

"You want me to play Beethoven?" Miles asks me. His tone is distant. He seems to be finding it hard to look at me.

"Yes." I point at the keyboard. "Can you do that?"

Miles nods sourly and sits down at the keyboard. First he plays the wrong notes. I'm about to suggest fetching the music box, but then the right tune begins to flow from his fingers.

If we ever get out of here, I'll never be able to listen to that song again. It will always remind me of this scene: my hand in the bloody bandage and Miles not daring to look at me. Mint and Alissa not talking to each other, and that lock of Caitlin's hair on the floor of the next room. Cleo has completely torn us apart.

The key to the last room is in a drawer that slides out of the keyboard as soon as Miles has finished playing. He goes back to Alissa in the doctor's office. It's too painful for the four of us to be together.

I no longer feel the adrenaline when we find something new. I just feel empty and numb.

The last room turns out to be a living room. There's a bookcase, a table with five chairs, and a saggy sofa, and there's an open kitchen. There are candles on the table, with hardened wax spilling into their holders.

Mint hurries to the windows, but they're fake, of course, with a brick wall behind them.

I try to imagine other people who have done this Escape Room. They gave their experience five stars. Would I have done the same if Cleo hadn't been here? Maybe.

I sit down on the sofa, feeling exhausted and dizzy.

What does it feel like when you're dying from blood loss? I think you lose consciousness first, and then you drift away until your heart stops beating.

Does it hurt?

"Can I light the candles?"

"Later. Okay?"

Those voices again. I can't take it anymore. I try to tune them out, but then the intercom falls silent.

I look at Mint, who is picking up each of the candles in turn and looking underneath them.

What are we actually hoping to find?

Cleo won't let us go. She's going to let me bleed to death in here.

I think about the key Mint and I found in Lia's room. What little hope we had has disappeared.

And then I remember the conversation I didn't get to finish with Mint just before we lifted up the floorboard.

"You never finished telling me about your fight with Alissa and Miles. . . ."

Mint is searching the rest of the living room. She ignores my comment.

"Mint?"

Mint looks at me. "Just leave it."

"Why?"

"You won't believe me anyway. Certainly not now."

"Because I'm in love with him, you mean?"

Will I ever get used to saying it out loud?

"Exactly." Mint sighs. "Miles threatened me. He put his hand on my throat and pressed with his thumb. Here." Mint points at a place on her throat. "He told me not to go shooting my mouth off to Alissa about what I saw."

It's all too much for me.

"He tried to strangle you?"

"He threatened me," says Mint. "He's smart enough not to leave any marks."

Is this about the same Miles I know? Mint's right. I don't believe her.

Miles is calmness itself. He never gets mad, even at the pizzeria when something goes wrong with an order. On a busy day, when everyone else is stressed out, he keeps his cool. I've never heard him curse or raise his voice.

"Yesterday I saw him flip out at someone who was walking past."

I try to picture it, but I can't do it.

"That someone was Cleo."

I feel a shiver run down my back, but oddly it's dripping with sweat at the same time. My hand is throbbing with pain.

"I don't want to hurt you." Mint comes to sit next to me. I look at her short hair. She let Alissa cut it to save my so-called girlfriend. Mint always does everything for everyone else. Why would she lie about this? I think she's terrified of Miles.

Then I remember the way he looked at me when I said I liked him. Miles's eyes were so cold that I thought I'd never feel warm again. I could imagine *that* Miles getting mad. *That* Miles could definitely have threatened Mint. And apparently he's met Cleo before.

"We need to get Alissa away from him."

Mint looks at me in surprise. "But she doesn't believe me. There's no point."

"I know." I feel dizzy, but I blink it away. This isn't the moment to die. I have to keep fighting. "But we'll do it anyway."

ALISSA

I can't take this anymore.

Sky lied about Caitlin.

Mint's lying about Miles.

They're both liars.

When I stand up, I see Miles looking, but he doesn't ask where I'm going. Which is just as well, as I don't think I'd dare tell him.

I close the door of Lia's room behind me. My bladder's sore. I've been needing to pee ever since we got here.

The round rug seems to be grinning at me. I can't just squat down here, can I?

The thought of Cleo watching me makes me desperately nervous.

I can't do it. It means losing my last bit of dignity.

In the far corner, I slip down my panties, hoping it's out of Cleo's sight.

It takes a moment, but then my pee splashes down onto the wooden floor.

* * *

"What's up?" Miles asks when I come back.

I don't want to talk. I want to feel like I did last night when we were sitting on his bed.

I want to feel like myself again, just for a moment.

"Kiss me." I look at him and pull him into the corner of the room. "Please."

It has everything, but it's never enough.

MINT

Miles and Alissa are kissing in the doctor's office. Sky's face darkens, and I quickly take hold of his good hand to let him know he doesn't have to do this alone.

"Let her go." Sky is the first to speak. "Now."

Miles and Alissa look up at the same moment, surprise on their faces.

"Sorry?" says Miles. "What's it got to do with you?"

"You threatened Mint."

Sky is the same old bulldozer as ever. And it works, because Miles is blinking nervously.

"That's not true."

"Mint told me everything." Sky looks at Alissa. "Why don't you believe her?"

"She's lying." Alissa looks at me. "You're both lying."

There's no point. Alissa doesn't want to believe us. We've been friends for years, but apparently that's nothing compared to this boy she's known for just a week.

It's because of Miles. He's so good at playing this game. If I were Alissa, I'd believe him too. There's something charismatic about Miles.

Bang! Another plastic ball falls into the room.

149

I bet Cleo's wanting to throw some more oil onto the fire. I'm too tired to ask what it says. Alissa is the only one who bothers to read the note.

Her eyes dart over the lines, and then she looks at me. She has a strange expression on her face that I've never seen before. Then she turns to Miles and takes his hand. She places the plastic ball and the note on the desk and walks past us. I want to stop her. I want to say that she's my best friend, even after everything that's happened tonight. And that I'm sorry I slapped her, but I only did it because I had no choice. And I'm sometimes jealous of her, it's true, but I'd never spread lies about Miles.

But I can't anymore. I feel defeated.

I hear Alissa closing the door of the boy's room behind her and Miles. Now it's two against two. If we ever get out of this Escape Room, it won't be as friends.

I can feel tears stinging my eyes again. I don't care now if Cleo sees me crying. Nothing matters anymore.

"Mint . . ." Sky's voice comes from a long way off.

I wipe my eyes on my sleeve, but they fill right up with tears again.

"Look at Cleo's message." Sky holds the strip of paper in front of my face.

> You guys really have no clue.
> I'm not the only one spying on you.
> It's nice to have an accomplice, you see.
> As I already wrote, Miles is with me.

150

ALISSA

"You okay?" Miles puts his arms around me. His embrace suddenly feels like this Escape Room, something I can't escape from. My heart is thumping so hard that I'm scared Miles will hear it.

It can't be true. Can it?

Miles pushes me away a little. "You're breathing so fast."

"Just give me a second." I look away, scared that he'll see how frightened of him I am. If he's really with Cleo, then he's at least as crazy as her, maybe even crazier. The whole time he's kept up the pretense that he was on our side. He made me believe that he liked me.

Or . . . Cleo's lying. She must be. She's trying to drive us all apart; that must be it.

Miles isn't a fake.

But then my gaze comes to rest on the photos.

On the dresser, among a few other frames, there's a gold one with a photograph of a blond girl.

It must be Lia, of course.

But why does she seem so familiar?

I've seen this girl before. But that's impossible, isn't it?

151

A razor-sharp image: that photograph, in a brightly colored frame, surrounded by other pictures. On a bookshelf . . .

Julie's bookshelf.

Then I look more closely at the other photographs and recognize someone else. There's a couple in a photograph with a wooden frame. The man has dark hair and eyes that look exactly like another pair of eyes I know.

I realize that I'm holding my breath.

The man in the photo is Miles's dad.

MILES

Has Alissa recognized the photos? She walks to the door and locks it. She stands there with her back toward me, so I can't see her face.

"What are you doing?" I ask.

It's a while before she answers.

"I don't want to see them again."

I feel a tingle in my stomach. She believes *me*. She's chosen *me*.

I think about the note in my pocket. As soon as we get out of here, I'll have to destroy it. Alissa must never get to read it.

When Cleo wrote that I was with her, I couldn't believe it. Why did she betray me? Was it because I'd agreed with Alissa when she said that Cleo was really sick?

I think about Sky's hand. That was when I knew Cleo would go much further than she'd promised. I can't stop her now. Everything's happening so quickly. Caitlin, Mint's hair, Sky's secret . . .

All that matters now is Alissa's safety. I have to make sure Cleo doesn't do anything to harm her.

I sit on the bed. The details of this room are so scarily good that I have to look really hard to spot the differences.

This is my room, but at the same time it's not.

It's a set.

Alissa is standing by the photos again. I need her to get away from there as quickly as possible.

"I'm sorry about your friends," I say to distract her.

"Friends are shit," she says quietly.

When we're out of here, she'll eventually forget Mint and Sky. I didn't want it to happen that way, but Mint ruined everything.

If she hadn't seen me in the meadows, if she'd kept her mouth shut, she'd still have Alissa as a friend.

But Mint is a troublemaker. She's just like Peyton, Karla's best friend. Peyton gossiped about me when she thought I couldn't hear her. "It's like Miles doesn't have any emotions." Those were Peyton's exact words. "He hasn't cried even once about what happened."

What I really wanted to do was to make her shut up, but instead I just stood and listened. Karla said that I was struggling, that I wasn't a talker. She stuck up for me, but I still felt insecure. I knew it was only a matter of time before Karla would bring it up with me again.

And that last afternoon on my bed, she asked how my therapy was going. If I felt that I could talk to the therapist about everything.

She asked at completely the wrong moment. All I was wearing was my boxer shorts, and she was lying under me with her shirt unbuttoned.

"You know me" was my simple answer.

"You have to talk," Karla said. "To me too."

"I can think of better things to do." I tried to kiss the subject away, but Karla pushed me off.

"You're not doing well. I can see that!"

"I'm doing fine."

"So why do you always keep your mirror covered?"

I looked at my wardrobe, with the towel hanging over the mirror.

"What do you want?"

Karla sat up. "I want to know what you're thinking."

She really didn't want to know that. I didn't even want to know that myself.

I pulled my T-shirt over my head. "I'm not thinking much."

"There's no need to be embarrassed." Karla placed her soft hand on my cheek. "I'm here for you."

I melted at her touch. "Don't . . ."

"There was nothing you could do, Miles."

I needed Karla to stop talking. It felt like my blood was made of soda water. It was bubbling and fizzing.

"I know you feel guilty, but you shouldn't. You have to move on. I know that you—"

"You don't know anything!"

Karla was startled by my loud voice.

"You still have both of your parents, so don't tell me to move on, because I have nowhere to move forward to. There's only back."

I knew I should stop, but a waterfall of words came pouring from my mouth.

155

"I disgust myself. Okay? I'm disgusted by my perfect face, without any scars. And I'm mad at you because you still want me, even after everything."

Karla did up the buttons of her shirt, her fingers shaking. Her bright-red bra, my favorite, disappeared from sight. And, for some reason, that made me even madder.

"I murdered my father. You know I did. I'm a murderer."

Karla grabbed her shoes from the floor and started walking toward the door. Desperately, I clasped my hand around her wrist.

"You're staying here."

"You're hurting me." Karla pulled away from me and headed out into the hallway.

"You wanted me to talk, didn't you?" I was right on her heels. "Well, now I'm talking!"

She was going to leave. I had to stop her. I ran after her, blocked the way. Her eyes darted from the front door to me and back again. There was nowhere she could go.

"Let me go."

"Where to?" I realized I was panting. "To see Peyton? So you can gossip about me again?"

Karla's face froze. Now she knew I'd been eavesdropping on them, and that made her furious.

"I should have listened to her. You really are disturbed."

I grabbed hold of Karla. It happened so quickly. In a flash, my hand was around her throat. I pressed my thumb into her skin.

Even before I realized what I was doing, a sharp pain went

through my shin. Karla had kicked me. I let go of her, and she ran to the front door.

"No!" I clawed at her clothes. We fell through the door together and onto the floor outside the apartment.

"Everything okay here?" The neighbor came outside. Karla stormed to the elevator. I watched her go, and I knew I'd lost her for good.

I look at the comforter under my hands. This was the same comforter I had on my bed on the day it all went wrong.

Then I hear the sound of breaking glass.

SKY

"It's locked." Mint looks at me, panic on her face.

I want to say it'll all be fine, but how can I say that when I don't believe it myself?

Alissa is in there, with him.

Miles is with Cleo.

All that time when I liked him, he was with her.

Was he the one who made sure I found the flyer? Must be.

I'm reeling, but if I sit down now, it'll feel like I'm abandoning Alissa.

Mint looks at me with big eyes. "Alissa locked the door herself! That's why she gave us that strange look. She's trying to protect us."

ALISSA

Miles's mind seems to be elsewhere. If I want to do it, it has to be *now*.

With my elbow, I nudge the wooden frame with the photo of Miles's dad. It falls, and the glass shatters on the wooden floor.

"What are you doing?" asks Miles.

I quickly bend down to pick up the shards of glass. "Just an accident."

I look at the biggest piece, which is half under the dresser. That's the one I want.

"Careful," Miles warns me. "You don't want to cut yourself."

All that time, I didn't notice anything. I thought he really liked me.

I reach for the shard of glass. The tip is razor sharp, just as I'd hoped.

I stand up with the shard behind my back and the photograph in my other hand. I have to know who Miles is, why he's doing all this.

"Who's that?"

Miles looks at the photo, and I see that he's startled. "What . . . what do you mean?"

"Well, the man's your dad, but who's the woman?"

A muscle in Miles's temple starts twitching. He doesn't say a word, but that tells me everything. I've driven him into a corner. There's nowhere he can go.

"That's supposed to be Lia." I point at the photograph of the young blond girl, which is still on the dresser. "I saw it at your mom's place too, on the bookshelves. So what's that photo doing here, in this Escape Room? Why is there a photo of your dad here? How do you know Cleo? Who *are* you, Miles?"

Miles's eyes narrow. "Julie isn't my mom."

His words hang in the room, like a thick fog.

"Julie's my aunt. That . . ." Miles points at the photo in my hand. "That's my mom. She's dead too."

I don't get it. That's impossible. I went to Miles's house. Julie introduced herself as his mother. Or maybe that's just what I thought because that's how things should be: children live with their parents.

"This is my old room," Miles says, looking around. "My bedroom in our old house. My mom was a family doctor, and my little sister, Lia, wanted to be a ballerina. Cleo's copied our entire house."

I can hardly breathe. Miles is making it worse by the second. What's he saying now?

Cleo and Miles. Miles and Cleo. What's their connection? Somehow I already know the answer, but it won't get through to me.

"Who is Cleo?" I ask anxiously.

Miles looks right at me. "Cleo's my sister."

160

"Who is Cleo?" It asks.
I hold my breath.
Will he finally choose me?
"Cleo's my sister."
The word is out.
Was that so hard, little brother?

ALISSA

Cleo is Miles's sister.

Now I remember the photo of Julie and a friend, sitting outside a café with two huge ice cream sundaes. That wasn't a friend in the photo. It was Cleo. She had dark hair back then, like Miles. She must have bleached it later. Otherwise I'd probably have recognized her at the entrance to the Escape Room.

I remember Miles pulling me in here. I thought he was doing it to help me, but he was just making sure that Cleo could carry out her plan.

"I want to explain it to you," Miles says, standing up.

By reflex, I take the shard of glass from behind my back and point it at him. "Don't come a step closer!"

Miles puts his hands up. "Okay, okay, calm down. . . ."

"You let Sky's hand get hurt. You let Mint's hair be cut."

Miles looks at me in despair. "I had no idea Cleo would go that far. I really didn't! I only came along to protect you. Don't you get it?"

"Why us? What do you guys want from us?"

"Not 'us.'" Miles looks down at his feet. "Mint and Sky are collateral damage."

I hold the piece of glass in front of me. "What do you mean?"

Miles takes a deep breath. "It was all about you from the start."

MILES

Cleo wanted to scare Alissa. Just to scare her. That's what she told me.

But then Sky's hand got trapped in the hatch. I thought at first that it was an accident, until I realized that my sister had started a completely different game, all by herself.

I couldn't go back. I was locked up, just like the rest of them.

"About me?" Alissa gasps. "What did I ever do to you?"

I knew Alissa only from Cleo's stories. Cleo had been following her for months, and she kept talking about the documentary with Alissa's interview. I didn't want to watch the documentary. I wanted to leave the past alone.

But Cleo couldn't do that. She became fixated on Alissa, and then she came up with a plan to get her to the Escape Room.

It was pure chance that I got to know Alissa. It was only when she introduced herself to me that I realized this was the girl my sister had been talking about for months.

And I liked Alissa right from the very first second. There was nothing I could do about it. She touched something inside me, and that hadn't happened since Karla.

I tried to talk Cleo out of the plan, but she wouldn't listen to me.

She kept repeating that it was a sign that I'd met Alissa, that it meant it should all go ahead.

And then Alissa called to ask if I'd go with them to the Escape Room. Cleo had left the flyer at the pizzeria, and Sky had found it.

What was I supposed to do?

All I could do was go along, in the hope that Cleo would rein herself in if I was there.

I had to go, so that I could protect Alissa. I needed to make sure all three of them got out safely.

Over the past year, Julie had warned me about Cleo several times. She said my sister was confused, that she needed help. But Cleo's over eighteen. She can decide for herself, and she didn't want any help.

She was a genius at fooling the social workers, smiling at all the right moments, and getting away with everything. She convinced our doctor that she was fine, that she was even thinking of resuming her studies.

But I knew she wasn't fine. Cleo retreated more and more to her dorm room. When I was there, all she talked about was Alissa, or about the Escape Room, where she had a part-time job. The people there thought her ideas for the Happy Family were so good that they actually built the room.

"Wait until you see it, little brother," she said. "All of the details are just right."

I never told Julie what Cleo was up to. If she found out that Cleo was having a replica of our house built . . .

I couldn't betray Cleo. She is my sister, after all.

165

She's the only other one left of our family. Dad, Mom, Lia—they're all dead.

"You're alive," I say to Alissa. "*That* is what you did to us."

I don't want to talk about this. It physically hurts. But Alissa needs to understand why Cleo's doing this.

"Our old house doesn't exist anymore," I say. "Everything's gone. Burned down."

Alissa's eyes widen. I can see that the cogs inside her head are starting to turn. And then I have to tell her. The story that my psychologist is so eager to hear, the story that Julie's been trying to drag out of me for months.

"I was out the night when it all went wrong. Dad told me to be home by ten, because it was Christmas Eve and he wanted us to be together. I thought it was dumb. Ten o'clock was for little kids. And I was seventeen.

"We went out dancing: Karla; her best friend, Peyton; and me. I was mad at Dad because of the fight we'd had before I left the house. The three of us got blind drunk.

"When I finally headed home at twelve, there were clouds of smoke above the houses. I remember thinking it was exciting. I even sped up. But when I got to our street, it turned out that it was our house that was on fire. I instantly sobered up.

"I ran to the fence, and a firefighter held me back. He shouted that his buddy was inside, and that I should wait outside. He asked me how many people were in the house, and I told him four. Cleo had already moved into a dorm room, but she was at home that night because of the holidays.

"It was driving me crazy, waiting there. The flames were licking the bricks, and there was smoke everywhere.

"Cleo came out. She had a big burn on her neck, and she was leaning on a firefighter. She was coughing, and she fell into my arms. She said she had to go back, that Lia had been calling for help. The firefighter shook his head.

" 'You guys stay here. We'll help your family,' he said, and he went back. His buddy went with him. I watched them run into the burning house.

"As Cleo was helped into the ambulance, the inferno spread.

"It was so incredibly hot where I was standing, but it didn't even occur to me to move away.

"Cleo came back. She'd fought her way out of the ambulance, and she had a blanket around her shoulders.

"I held my sister. I was scared she was going to run back inside for Lia. And at that moment . . . something collapsed. My mom and dad's bedroom, I think. The neighbors standing around us were screaming and shouting, but Cleo and I were both silent.

"More firefighters went into the house. They were shouting, but I didn't know the names. And then a man came out. The same man who had brought Cleo out. The man who had promised to help our family. His whole face was black. He could barely stand. The ambulance guy gave him an oxygen mask.

"The firefighters didn't do anything else after that. All their attention went to the other fireman. Dad, Mom, Lia were forgotten."

"M-my dad . . . ," stammers Alissa. "That man was my dad."

I look up. "So now you get it."

It's deadly silent in the room.

I see Cleo again, standing with me behind the fence. She collapsed, clung on to me like a child to its mother. I had to keep standing, for her. But I was tired, so tired.

"My dad lost a good friend that night." Alissa's voice is trembling. "He was ill for months. I told you that."

"He should have let Cleo and me go inside," I say. "We knew the house. We could have saved them."

Alissa doesn't say another word. Tears are streaming down her cheeks. Cleo's always been way angrier than me. Particularly when Alissa appeared in that documentary. It was like Alissa was a flame near a gas leak. Cleo exploded.

"She's acting like she's the victim of what happened that night," Cleo had screamed. "But her dad's just sick. At least she still *has* a father! She doesn't wake up sweating every night because she can hear her sister crying out for help, and there's nothing she can do. She doesn't have a scar on her neck that reminds her of what happened every day."

I tried to calm my sister down, but she just got madder. Especially when I said I didn't want to watch the documentary.

"They're your family too, or have you forgotten them? Just like all those firefighters did?"

"Of course not."

"That's not how it seems." Cleo's eyes were spitting fire. "You've just traded them in for Julie!"

I knew it was her grief talking, but Cleo went too far. I left, and we didn't speak for two weeks.

Cleo seemed to have calmed down after that, and we left the subject of Alissa alone. We did fun things together again. Cleo gave me my first driving lesson, and now and then I delivered a pizza for free. For a little while, it felt like we'd been before the accident.

But when I was over at Cleo's one day, I saw a notebook on the windowsill. Cleo had gone to the bathroom, and I opened the book out of curiosity. There were all kinds of notes in it that didn't seem to make sense at first.

Has two brothers and a sister. Sister the same age as Lia.

As I read Lia's name, my breath stopped, and I read on frantically.

It has everything. It's beautiful. No scars. Dad's still a firefighter.

So Cleo was keeping notes about this Alissa. It was full of recent dates. She was still obsessed.

"What are you doing?" Cleo was suddenly back in the room. "That's mine!"

I looked at my sister. "You're following her."

"So?" Cleo snatched the book from my hands.

"You have to stop this."

"Why?" Cleo looked at me venomously. "Somebody has to do it."

"Come live with us," I begged her. "You know Julie won't mind."

Cleo laughed. "You think? She doesn't even want you to come see me on your own. Does she know you're here now?"

I felt myself blushing, because she was right. Julie didn't know. She wanted to be around when I saw Cleo, because she knew how mad Cleo was about the past.

"You see." Cleo crossed her arms. "Julie doesn't understand us. She lost her brother that night, but we lost way more."

I crossed my arms too. "I'm not getting involved."

Cleo came to stand in front of me. "Again? Like you didn't get involved that night?"

That hurt. If I'd come home earlier, I could have saved my sister, because Lia's bedroom was next to mine. Maybe I'd have found the fire sooner, because I often had to go pee at night. The fire was started by a candle on a table, which Lia had lit. My little sister always wanted to have candles around, and Mom must have missed that one when they went to bed. The candle was too close to the curtains. They caught fire after everyone had gone to bed.

I look up at Alissa, who is still standing in front of me with the shard of glass. Maybe it should all end here for me. Perhaps it's better that way.

I let my mom and dad and my sister burn. I drove Karla away. I let Cleo have her way. . . .

Why didn't I talk to Julie? She might have been able to stop Cleo.

But Cleo's my sister. Other than Julie, she's the only family I still have. I couldn't betray her.

"Do you want to stab me?" I spit out the words. "Then do it!"

170

"Don't come any closer." Alissa holds out the piece of glass, trembling. "I'll do it. I really will do it."

I murdered my own father.

And my mother, and my sister.

Lia, who always wanted me to play the keyboard for her. I'd play until I had blisters on my fingers if only it would bring her back.

"Don't move." Alissa's voice is shaking. She holds out the glass farther. "I'm warning you, Miles."

"Just do it," I beg her. "Please. It's what I want. It's what I deserve."

"No!" Alissa's voice is an octave higher than normal. "Don't move!"

There's a bang on the door. Mint and Sky are tired of waiting. They've come to rescue Alissa.

"You're lucky to have friends like that," I hear myself saying, and I reach out my arms to Alissa.

It happens so quickly that I don't realize at first. But then I feel a sharp, stabbing pain.

"No!"

I swipe everything off the desk in one movement.

On the screen, I see Miles lying motionless on the floor.

I hear Lia's voice inside my head again.

She begged for help that night.

Everyone abandoned her.

That firefighter promised to help her, but he didn't think she was important enough.

After all, he had his own daughter at home.

He had It.

MINT

"No! Don't move!" Alissa's high-pitched voice comes through the door.

I don't think about it for a second, but bash my shoulder into the door, which swings opens with a bang. As I fly into the room, I take in everything at once.

Miles is lying on the floor. Alissa is standing at his feet. She's shaking so much that it's as if I can see two of her. She's holding her hands away from her, like they're covered in something dirty.

But then I see Miles's stomach. In the place where I've had stabbing pains for the past week, there's a piece of glass sticking out. His gray T-shirt is red with blood.

"Alissa . . ."

She doesn't react. When I grab hold of her, she looks up with a wild expression. Her blue eyes look pleadingly at me, as if I'm the only one who can help her. That's what Sky looked like earlier this evening too, but I don't know if there's anything I can do for her.

"Take her with you," I say to Sky, who's staring wide-eyed at Miles.

I push them into the hallway, toward the living room. When

they're gone, I look at Miles, who is still lying there without moving.

What happened here?

Alissa clearly stabbed him, but was it self-defense?

Is he dead?

I have to make sure he can never come anywhere near us again. Never again.

I roll the desk chair into the hallway and am about to close the door, but I can't do it. I can't leave Miles behind like that, can I? That would make me even worse than Cleo, and I don't want that.

I step back into the room. Maybe I should pull the glass out of his stomach. Or will that make it bleed even more?

As I go closer, I see Miles's eyelids trembling.

So he's still alive. I don't know whether to be relieved or not.

Then a strange rattling sound comes from his mouth, and he opens his eyes. He looks at me, dazed. A crooked grin appears on his face, as if only the right half of his body is still working.

"Hey . . . ," I hear him say quietly.

Miles tries to get up, but winces.

"You have to stay lying down," I say, "or your organs will be even more damaged."

"Does that matter?" Miles makes that strange sound again, and his eyes roll back.

Shocked, I lean forward, but then I hear his shallow breathing. He's fainted, but he's still alive.

I look at the piece of glass sticking out of his stomach. What organs might it have hit? His intestines?

I think about the anatomical model we put together at the beginning of the evening. I managed to get everything in the right place in one go, but now I can't remember which organ went where.

I take a deep breath and stand up. I can't help Miles. Like the rest of us, he'll have to wait for Cleo to open the door.

I push the desk chair under the door handle and check that it's sturdy enough. Even though Miles doesn't have the strength to stand up, let alone to smash down a door.

In the living room, I go sit with my friends. Alissa is sitting in the middle, between Sky and me. I exchange a quick glance with Sky. His face is ashen.

"Cleo is Miles's sister," I hear him say.

I don't want to know. I don't want to know exactly who that boy with the glass in his stomach is. I just want it all to stop.

I take hold of Alissa's wounded, trembling hands—and that's when I notice that mine are shaking too.

We don't talk. What is there to say?

All we can do is wait and hope for a miracle.

He is dead.
It murdered my little brother.
I throw open the door to the corridor.

CAITLIN

She's going away.

That disturbed witch is really going away.

I try to move my hands, but that just makes the ropes cut even more deeply into my skin.

There's a telephone on the floor, an old-fashioned one with a cord, almost within reach. The receiver is next to it. I can hear the dial tone.

I need to hurry. She could be back at any minute.

I twist my hands this way and that. The ropes hurt so much. It feels like I'm tearing my skin open until it bleeds.

But slowly they loosen. I could cry with relief, even though my eyes feel so dry and raw from all the crying I've already done.

On one of the screens, I see Sky. The boy who broke my heart twice tonight. First, because he never really loved me, and second because I can see him suffering.

Did that woman mess him up like that?

I'm free.

I look in surprise at my hands, as if they belong to someone else.

I have to hurry.

With shaking fingers, I pick up the phone and call the emergency number. A woman answers.

"Where are you calling from and what help do you require?"

I tell them the name of the town and ask for the police and the ambulance.

"Someone's been hurt," I say. "Really badly, and I . . ."

There's a click. The woman's putting me through.

"Wait!" I call, but there's another voice. This time it's a man.

"Where exactly are you?"

"In an Escape Room. But I can't remember the name of the street. Please. You have to come."

"Do you remember anything else? There are three Escape Rooms in town."

Three? I think frantically. I came here on my bike. I leaned it against one of the buildings. They were old houses. The street had a bird's name, a . . .

"Gull!" I almost scream it. "Gull Street!"

"That's great. So now we know where you are. What happened?"

"A member of the staff has gone crazy. Someone got stabbed. . . ."

"How many people have been injured?"

"I don't know. Please. You have to hurry."

"How old are the victims?"

"No idea. Between fifteen and eighteen. Something like that?" I start crying again. "I'm so scared."

"Help's on the way."

I look at the screens. That boy, Miles, he's still lying on his back, absolutely still. He hasn't moved since he spoke to Mint. Alissa's sitting there as if she's stunned. Sky is hugging his injured hand, and Mint's lips are moving but she's not making any sound. It's like watching a movie, but I know the actors.

Suddenly I see movement on another screen, one that nothing's happened on all night. It's the camera at the entrance to the Escape Room.

Cleo is opening the door. I can hardly believe it, but the black-and-white pictures don't lie. Is she letting everyone go? That means this nightmare is finally over.

But then Cleo throws a bottle into the room. There's something wrapped around it. A cloth? The whole screen suddenly flashes bright white, as if I'm looking into the sun.

"No . . . ," I groan.

"What did you say?" asks the man on the other end of the line.

The normal picture returns. I see flames flickering around the desk and the anatomical model with the organs.

"Fire . . ." I gasp for breath. "She's set the place on fire!"

"Can you get to safety, miss?"

I drop the receiver and start running.

SKY

There's the sound of breaking glass, a muffled explosion. I smell burning.

"Fire," I whisper.

"Come on." Mint leads Alissa and me to the far corner of the kitchen. She turns the tap. No water comes out. Everything here is fake.

"Here." I take three dish towels off a shelf. "Hold these over your mouth and nose. It'll help against the smoke. Stay with Alissa. I'm going to go take a look."

As I walk to the doctor's office, I can see six doors instead of three, and I have to lean against the wall so that I don't collapse.

The heat coming from the doctor's office is overwhelming. When I see the flames, I know there's no way out. We can't even reach the door.

How can such a big fire develop so quickly?

Cleo wants to murder us.

Was that her plan all along?

Did she just want to play with us a bit before burning us alive?

I see the desk chair up against the door of the boy's room.

Mint has locked Miles up. Quiet Mint, who didn't dare to talk to Miles last week in the park. Mint, the mousiest girl in school. The same Mint who left Miles in there to bleed out.

The flames are licking at the walls of the hallway. They'll soon reach the boy's room. Does Miles really deserve to die this way? Alone and with a shard of glass in his stomach?

I know that Cleo's his sister, and that it's partly because of him that we're in here, but I feel sorry for him. I hate it, but somewhere inside me, there's still a remnant of love. Maybe it will never go away.

I take the chair away from the door and pull it open. Miles is still lying on the floor. His face is gray. A pool of blood has spread over the wooden floor.

It's just like I'm watching a movie, as if this isn't real. I curse. Miles and I are both bleeding to death, but it'll happen sooner to him. Alissa pushed the piece of glass deep into his stomach.

I hurry to Miles and tap his cheek. He doesn't react, but when I put my fingers on his throat, I feel a faint pulse.

I put Miles's arm around my shoulders and struggle to lift him to his feet.

Miles groans, but his eyes remain shut. I see more blood gushing from the wound.

How am I going to do this? This would be difficult if I were in peak condition, but with just one good hand it's almost impossible.

The whole room is spinning.

My hand feels as if it's already on fire.

I stagger along the hallway, with the flames at my heels. With

Miles like a heavy rag doll by my side, I stumble back to the living room. As soon as Mint sees him, she explodes at me.

"What are you doing?!"

Alissa moves closer to the wall, as if she wants to disappear into it. I lay Miles on the kitchen floor. He groans again when his head hits the tiles.

"We can't just leave him there to die."

I don't want to become an animal in here. I want to remain Sky until the final second.

MINT

Someone starts crying.

Is it me?

We're holding each other's hands.

All I can do is look at Miles. It's like he's laid out for his funeral, so peaceful and quiet.

How will I look soon?

Will Mom and Dad ever go to church again at Christmas? Or will they stop because I should be sitting between them?

I see our house in front of me, my room. The bulletin board with the photos of Sky, Alissa, and me. I'm always standing kind of hidden behind my friends, with Alissa looking radiant at the front.

I rub the short spikes on my scalp. Will my mom and dad recognize me like this? Or will I soon be burned so badly that they won't be able to tell the four of us apart? A sob escapes my throat.

The smoke curls under the door.

Caitlin's gone.

In the place where I tied her up, there's just the rope now.

"Hello?"

I look around, but no one's there.

Where did that voice come from?

Then I see the receiver lying next to the phone.

"Are you still there?"

I put the receiver to my ear.

"Who is this?" I ask.

"Emergency services."

I flinch.

There's a loud bang.

On the screens, I see people coming into the building.

They're coming for me.

ALISSA

"Hang in there, guys!"

I open my eyes. The room is full of smoke. My eyes are stinging.

Is it the intercom? Who's speaking this time? Lia? Miles? Their mom or dad?

Is this a new game?

But I can't take any more.

Cleo has to stop.

"We're nearly there, Alissa!"

I know that voice.

It's Dad.

Am I dead?

But then what's Dad doing here?

There's a bang, loud voices, a strange hiss.

Even more smoke.

"Alissa!"

"Dad?" I croak, taking the dish towel from my mouth.

"They're alive!" someone shouts. They're cheering. Why would they be happy? There's no reason at all to be happy. I murdered someone.

"I . . ." I have to tell them. Everyone needs to know what I've done. "Miles. I . . ."

Then I'm picked up, and I feel a hard edge against my cheek. It takes me a moment to realize what it is: Dad's fire helmet.

THIS

IS

WHERE

IT

ENDS

SKY

The wheels of the gurney fold in as I'm lifted into the ambulance. I only notice now that I'm not holding Mint's and Alissa's hands anymore. When did I let go of them? They're still inside!

Mint, Alissa . . . I want to shout their names, but there's something over my mouth.

What's going on? I sit up, but a paramedic gently pushes me back onto the gurney.

"Your friends are okay."

I look around. Miles is lying beside me, with all kinds of wires attached to him and an oxygen mask over his mouth. That must be what I have too. That's why I can't talk.

"We gave your friend morphine for the pain. He's unconscious."

I want to say that Miles is anything but my friend, but then the ambulance starts moving, and a feeling of nausea washes over me.

"Just keep still," the man says to me.

Where's Caitlin? Is she still with Cleo?

I pull the oxygen mask off my face. The elastic pinches behind my ears. "Caitlin . . ."

"Keep still," the man says, a little more forcefully this time.

What if he's part of all this? Am I really in an ambulance, or is this some new Escape Room?

I try to move my fingers, but nothing happens. All I can feel is a tingling sensation where they should be.

What's happened to my fingers?

I have to drum. I have to . . .

MINT

"I'm staying with Alissa," I say to the police officer who wants to drive me to the hospital.

The woman from the ambulance nods. "Fine, but we need to leave now."

I climb in next to the gurney. Alissa's dad is already sitting by her head. He's stroking his daughter's hair nonstop.

"What happened, baby girl?" I hear him asking.

Maybe it's just as well they gave Alissa a strong sedative to calm her down, because I don't know if she could have answered his question.

Where should I start? I know the police are going to want us to tell them everything, but I don't know if I'll ever be able to talk about this. No one will understand what happened in the Escape Room. No one will understand what the four of us have been through.

No, the three of us.

I can't count Miles.

All that time, he was part of the sick plan.

"Mint." Alissa's dad rests his hand on mine. "I want to thank you."

I'm startled out of my thoughts. "What for?"

"For being such a good friend to my daughter."

You always want all the attention, even at your dad's expense!

I swallow. "I don't know about that."

"It's thanks to you that she's still alive. Putting those dish towels over your faces was a really good idea."

"That was Sky's idea."

I think of my best friend, who's in the other ambulance along with Miles. I don't find it reassuring that they've knocked Miles out with drugs. I think I'll always be on guard from now on.

"I'm sure it was a struggle for you in there too."

Alissa's dad runs his eyes over my scalp.

I'd almost forgotten my short fuzz.

"It was a struggle for all of us," I say quietly.

I look at Alissa, who stabbed Miles. If he doesn't make it, she'll be a murderer.

She's lying there peacefully now, but soon she'll wake up into this hell. I hope for her sake that she goes on sleeping for a while longer.

"Mint!" My mom's voice echoes along the corridor in the hospital. Her stiletto heels make a quick tapping sound. She comes running up, with my dad right behind her.

Alissa's gurney is pushed away. I feel two arms around me.

"Mom . . . ," I say quietly.

"Oh, sweetheart." My mom pulls away and her eyes fill with

tears. She holds out her hand and strokes my head. "What did they do to you?"

Another impossible question. If I tell her, she'll never let me out of the house again.

I look at my dad, who's standing there awkwardly. He's trying not to look at my head, but I can see that he's finding it difficult.

"Dad, I . . ."

My dad takes a step forward and hugs me to him. Mom does the same. It feels warm. I can't tell which arms are whose anymore. I can't move, but it's completely different from being locked up.

SKY

My mom's stopped crying, but I know she could start again at any minute. My dad's sitting silently by my bedside and looking at my hand, which is in a plaster cast. It has seventeen stitches, and it's broken in a few places too, but according to the doctor I'll be able to drum again eventually.

Now and then I fall asleep, but the nurse says that's a good thing. She keeps repeating how lucky we are. Alissa's dad and the other firefighters reached us just in time.

I think of the moment the smoke came curling under the door. I seriously thought I was going to die.

But every time I see my mom and dad, I realize I'm still alive.

I made it. She's right—I was lucky.

So why don't I feel lucky?

The nurse puts her head around the door. "There's a visitor for you."

I sit up a little in my pillows. "Mint?"

But it's Caitlin who comes into the room. She has black lines of mascara on her face, and she's fiddling with the ring on her little finger.

My heart starts racing, as if I'm back in the Escape Room.

"And who's this?" asks my dad.

"Caitlin," my mom says. "Sky's girlfriend."

I try to ignore the embarrassment, but I can see Caitlin blushing.

"Dad, Mom . . ." I look at them. I can tell they never want to leave my side again, but there's no way I'm having this conversation with them here.

"Okay. We're leaving," says my dad, pulling my mom out into the corridor.

As Caitlin sits down on my dad's chair, I stare at the blankets. I know I should say something, but where to begin?

"I'm sorry," we both say at the same time.

"Huh?" I look at Caitlin in surprise. "Why are *you* sorry?"

Caitlin glances at my hand. "That you had to go through that."

She's kind, far too kind.

"You heard all of it, didn't you?" I ask, just to make sure. "What was said in there?"

Caitlin blinks a few times. "I was in the same room as her."

"Did she do anything . . ."

"She tied me up, cut off a bit of hair, and scared me," Caitlin says, summing it up. "That was it."

"Isn't that enough?" I can feel tears welling up again. How am I ever going to make it up to her?

I want to take her hand, but remember too late that I'm supposed to be resting mine and feel a stab of pain.

"Ow."

"You okay?"

"You have to stop being so nice," I tell her. "Please, hate me, hit me, but don't be like this."

"I'd like to hit you," Caitlin says. "But I'll do it when you're better."

I notice that I'm smiling, which sends a tear trickling down my cheek and toward the pillow.

"I don't want you to see me cry."

"I get it." Caitlin gives my shoulder a gentle thump. "People might think you're gay."

I feel it bubbling up inside me, but it's Caitlin who's first to burst out laughing. Then I join in. We laugh way louder than we should. We laugh because we're still alive.

"Sky." Mint comes into my room and throws both arms around me. I just woke up. After Caitlin's visit, I went back to sleep. My mom and dad are sitting by my bed again. They look shocked when they see Mint's new hairstyle.

Mint holds me a few seconds longer, and I realize how much I like it.

"How's the pain?" she asks when she lets me go.

"Morphine," I say. "Miracle drug."

"Alissa's still sleeping," says Mint. "I'll go check on her soon."

I'd really like to go with her, but the nurse says I have to stay in bed.

"You bandaged me up better," I say when I see Mint looking at my hand. "You could get a job here, no problem."

"I've seen enough blood for now."

I give her a tentative smile.

"I just saw Caitlin out in the corridor," Mint says quietly. "Everything okay?"

"Sure is."

I want to ask her about Miles, but I don't dare with my mom and dad there. The police just told them the whole story. When my dad heard that Miles was involved, I was worried for a moment that he was about to go storming into Miles's room and give him a good kicking.

"Cleo's at the police station," says Mint. "They're interviewing her right now. And then it's *his* turn."

Crazy Mint, who always says everything at just the right moment.

She places a kiss on my forehead. "I'm going to go see Alissa."

I look at her short hair. She seems invincible. I hope she keeps it like that.

Mint goes out into the corridor. She's the only one who came out of this unharmed. But I know that her real wounds are inside.

She was called a shadow of Alissa. She was humiliated and threatened.

On a whim, I put my hand up to my mouth. I don't care that my mom and dad are sitting by my bed when I yell through the hospital: "Hey, if I weren't gay, I'd never fall in love with Alissa. It would be you!"

MILES

There's a stranger sitting by my bedside. When I peer at him out of the corner of my eye, I notice that his jacket is hanging open, and there's a gun in a holster on his belt.

I close my eyes again. As long as I pretend to be sleeping, no one will ask questions. Questions about Alissa, about my sister, about all the things that happened in there.

Alissa stabbed me. I thought she couldn't do it, but she could.

I wanted to protect her, but she didn't understand. She thought I was just as bad as my sister.

Cleo . . . Where is she now?

I don't know if I ever want to see her again.

There's a panicky voice in the corridor.

"Miles!"

Julie. I feel a lump in my throat and my eyes fill with tears. What's she doing here? Why does she still want to see me after all this?

"Sorry, ma'am. You can't go in there yet."

"Why not? He's family. He lives with me!"

"We understand that you want to speak to him, but we need to take his statement first."

"Statement?" Julie shouts. "He didn't do anything. This is all one big misunderstanding!"

I squeeze my eyes even more firmly shut.

ALISSA

Miles is standing in front of me, with those ice-blue eyes of his.

He takes a step forward. I stab him.

There's blood everywhere.

On the glass, on my hands, on my face.

"You're back." Mint's face is so close that I can hardly focus on it. "You're a champion sleeper, you know."

Where am I?

The hospital.

Still.

My dad stroked my hair. That was nice.

Mom cried. Even Koby and Ruben cried.

And Fenna? Was she there too?

Maybe Mom and Dad left her at home. That would be good. I don't want her to think I'm shipwrecked too.

"Your mom and dad are just talking to the doctor. They'll be back soon."

Mint lays a cool hand on my forehead. I look at her short hair and reach out to her face.

"I . . . I . . ."

"Yep. You gave me a new do." Mint nods. "It'll grow back. Or maybe I'll leave it like this."

"I hurt you," I say, completing my sentence.

"I can handle it," says Mint, but I hear a crack in her voice. All this time, she's been so brave, but now she's breaking.

We're both crying.

"Miles is alive," Mint says through her tears. When I hear his name, my heart rate shoots up. "He's being interviewed by the police, and so is Cleo. They want to speak to us too."

I don't know if I'll ever be able to talk about what happened in there. Words can't explain what it was like.

"You warned me about Miles, and I . . ."

There are so many things I want to say to Mint, but the words get stuck in my throat. I'm crying again. Will I ever shake off this feeling of powerlessness?

"I'll never be able to trust anyone again."

"Of course you will," says Mint quietly. "We have each other."

I close my eyes. The nightmare comes back: Miles, the glass, the blood . . . How am I ever supposed to live with those images?

"Alissa?" A voice startles me, a voice that makes me feel warm, deep inside.

Before I can even look up, a weight falls onto my chest. I feel hair tickling my face.

"Fenna!" Mom sounds stern. "Be gentle with your sister."

201

But I wrap my arms around Fenna and give her the biggest hug.

Over Fenna's shoulder, I see Mint smiling. She's right. The trust will come back. We have each other.

There's a way out of this Escape Room.

They all want to know why.
The press, the police, and Julie.
I'm not talking.
One day I'll write a book about it.
And then everyone will understand.
I did this for our family.
For Dad, Mom, Lia, and Miles.
They say my brother's alive,
but I don't think I'll see him for a while.
Julie will do everything she can to keep him
away from me.
Miles is the only one I have left.
I didn't know he was still alive in there.
I really didn't.
My plan worked.
I broke It.
I hope It never forgets what it's like to be powerless.
The police officer tells me what's in store for me.
I look outside.
The sun shines in through the bars.
The warmth on my face is pleasant.

For a moment, it's like I'm running through the park
again.
The sun on my face, and It on the bench.
My brother talking to It.
The opportunity that suddenly presented itself.
It was a sign.
People will eventually come to understand that,
won't they?
Because if you had one shot, one opportunity,
to seize everything you ever wanted
in one moment,
you wouldn't just let it slip, would you?

THIS

IS

WHERE

THE

AUTHOR

HAS

SOMETHING

TO

SAY

My first Escape Room was in Haarlem, the Netherlands.

When we went in, there was one member of the staff who explained the rules to us. He was going to watch everything that happened inside through the camera.

I made a joke and said to the others, "What if he never lets us go?" That joke was the basis of this book.

Escape Rooms have become an addiction for me. I plan to do as many as I can.

Although . . .

After this book, I'm extra careful.

I tell at least one person where I'm going, and I always say, "If you haven't heard from me by ten, then come rescue me."

You know, just to be sure.

Maren Stoffels

ABOUT THE AUTHOR

MAREN STOFFELS published her first book at age seventeen. She likes stories that are based on real experiences. Reading her books makes you feel like it could all happen to you. And maybe it will. . . .

marenstoffels.nl

GET **BOOKS** GET **PERKS** GET **INSPIRED**

GET
Underlined

**A Community of YA Book Nerds
& Aspiring Writers!**

READ

Book recommendations, reading lists, YA news

LIFE

Quizzes, book trailers, author videos

PERKS

Giveaways, merch, sneak peeks

CREATE

Community stories, writing contests and advice

We want to hear YOUR story!

Create an account to write original stories,
connect with fellow book nerds and authors, build
a personal bookshelf, and get access to content
based on your interests!

GetUnderlined.com
@GetUnderlined 🄵 🄾 🅈 🕭 ▶

1407

Want a chance to be featured? Use #GetUnderlined on social!